HELL'S ROAD

HELL'S ROAD

JUNGLE SERIES BOOK 2

Alan Berkshire

4 Horsemen
Publications, Inc.

4 Horsemen Publications, Inc.
1497 Main St. Suite 169
Dunedin, FL 34698
4horsemenpublications.com
info@4horsemenpublications.com

Cover by J. Kotick
Typesetting by Autumn Skye
Edited by Heather Teele

Library of Congress Control Number: 2022942599

Paperback ISBN-13: 978-1-64450-695-0
Audiobook ISBN-13: 978-1-64450-693-6
Ebook ISBN-13: 978-1-64450-694-3

For Stephen King

My inspiration

Contents

One

M25 ORBITAL

It was amazing. It really was. After all the shit of the last three days—the pain, the uncertainty, the violence—they gritted their teeth, squared their shoulders, and got on with the job at hand. I was proud to call them family. It also made me feel bitter. I had let them down ... badly. I had allowed evil into our ranks, and I hadn't even seen it coming. I was sick about Tina. I had failed her the most, and she had paid horribly for my defeat.

"No one could have seen it," Jules protested. "I was here, and he had me fooled."

"That's just it!" I argued. "I wasn't here, and I should have been, not on some fool's errand trying to find the impossible."

"Now you're talking nonsense," Jules spat. "We needed to find somewhere new to live, we still do, and you had to check out Thamesmead to make sure it was safe. Who knew what Kaminsky was planning?"

"And I gave him the perfect opportunity to do it," I said.

Derek "Rambo" Kaminsky had turned up at the Block out of the blue, roaring through the entrance arch on his Goldwing motorcycle, large as life and twice as cocky. As soon as I saw him, I knew he was trouble, but I ignored my instincts, allowing him into our community with disastrous results.

Yeah, he looked like Sly Stallone's character from a distance. That should have been a clue because the closer you got to Kaminsky, the more the illusion of resemblance faded. He was big but nowhere as muscular. He had the same mop of shoulder-length black hair, even tied back with a red bandana. But the eyes beneath the Rayban sunglasses were pale and washed-out, his mouth was thin and hard, blessed with a permanent sneer, and his nose was too big. He played us—played me. Though I am not one to bear a grudge, I hate him for it.

Beside me, Jules' dark eyes flashed in a dark face that belied his sixty-three years. The only real sign of old age was the peppering of grey in his tight, curly hair, which he wore cropped close to his narrow skull.

"There's no time for pointless recriminations. For now, done is done; we can all grieve later. Right now, we have to get out of here."

I had never heard his voice so cold and hard before. I think he was as angry as I was about being fooled; he just handled it better, though he blamed himself just as much.

"If what Williams told you is right, then we've got less than four days before London is turned into the world's biggest bonfire," he said tightly.

Standing on the rooftop of the Block, probably for the last time, I looked down into the courtyard fifty feet below us. People, our friends and family, were stacking suitcases in a neat pile just to the right of the archway entrance. The old bus we had used as a mobile gate was parked outside on the street. In its place was a bright blue coach with the name "Stamford" written on the side in gleaming gold livery. Our mechanic, Roger Boulton, had gone over the old London Transport single-decker bus and declared it inadequate for the long journey north. It was another brief moment of concern until Alan Holden and Jeff Shepherd, the Block's scavengers, rolled into the courtyard with the new coach, its horn blaring. I discovered later that Alan and Jeff had already been in conference with Roger about his concerns with the old bus. Of course, they had a solution to the problem. Weeks ago on one of their forays, they discovered a coach company only a few miles away. Their talent for acquisition never ceased to amaze me.

While the residents stacked their suitcases—a strict one per person—Alan, Jeff, and Roger set about fortifying the coach with some of the other men. Steel mesh, cannibalised from the lower windows of the Block, was bolted over the side windows of the vehicle, and more protective mesh covered the windscreen and rear windows, welded into place for added strength.

In a few brief hours, the coach was turned into a rolling fortress. It had been a Catch-22 situation: we couldn't really afford the time, but we couldn't risk driving out of the Block without adequate protection. The world was no longer safe; travelling was dangerous, and our small band of survivors needed to be protected at all costs. The black Dust had fallen, bringing lethal, sentient vines that were taking over our world, every piece of grassland, park, woodland, forest. They were slowly choking us out of existence. And with them came the hellish guardians: Creeps, ape-like creatures which grew and evolved at a terrifying rate. They were merciless, ruthless killers with no fear of death. Their sole aim was to protect the vines and exterminate every other living thing on the planet.

On the upside, the new coach was bigger than the old bus and far more comfortable with tons of storage space. It had a few extras which would prove invaluable on the trip: an on-board bathroom and for the kids—I suspect, some of the adults too—a DVD system that would occupy one and all.

Jules and I argued. We always argued but in a good way. He was my guide, my mentor, and my conscience, especially in times of doubt like now. We descended to the courtyard; it would soon be time to leave.

The men stood back, admiring their morning handiwork.

"Okay," said Roger, "that's all about we can do for the coach."

I looked up and down the length of the vehicle. It was an incredible job considering the limited time to accomplish it.

"The emergency exits are still accessible," continued Roger. "The sunroofs can be used as exits should the need arise."

We watched as the suitcases were loaded into the belly of the coach, packed tightly to maximise the space.

"We're going pack as much of the canned and dry food onto the coach as we can, some inside beneath the seats. At the rear of the storage space, we're going to load the fuel. It's a fine balance between fuel and food. Either way, it's not going to be enough and probably won't last very long."

"We'll scavenge as we go," Alan said as we walked across the courtyard toward our three transit vans.

"The short wheelbase van is going to be used to transport three generators." Jeff took up the narrative. "I'd like to take more, but we just haven't the room. We've got tools, fixings, nails, screws and the like, and a ton of other hardware. We've also loaded the weapons and ammunition on board. It seems we've built quite an armoury.

"The two long wheelbase vans are going to be loaded with food and water," Jeff continued. "It's all pretty basic with few luxuries, I'm afraid. We loaded biscuits, sweets, chocolate, and canned drinks onto the coach, mainly for the kids. Hopefully, we'll find more on our travels."

"What's happening there?" asked Jules, noting the activity around one of the other vans.

"Roof rack," Jeff said. "All the camping gear, tents, tarps, and cooking gear is going to be packed there with a steel mesh cover to keep it safe in case of attack. We've packed a couple of barbeques on the coach for use en route."

"It seems you've thought of everything," I said admiringly.

"We hope so," said Alan. "Once we leave, that's going to be it. Anything we may have forgotten, we'll have to find on the way or go without."

"If all three transits are loaded to the gills, how are you going to scavenge?" asked Jules.

Adam and Jeff grinned, sharing a secret joke. "Adam's taxi," they said in unison.

I laughed. "Well, to be honest, I was intending to leave it behind as surplus to requirements, but if you lads have a need for it, then it's yours and welcome."

"Most of this has been worked out on the fly," began Jeff, "but we have made certain assumptions."

"Go on," I said.

"Roger volunteered to ride Peter's motor-bike and act as our forward scout whilst Peter is recovering from his injuries."

I waited, already knowing what Jeff was getting at.

"We're not happy with Roger, or anyone, being out there on their own, and we were wondering what your friend..."

"Linda," I said.

"Yeah, Linda," Jeff continued. "We wondered if she was going to stay with us, and if so..."

"Would she be prepared to act as the other scout?" I finished for him.

"Yeah," said Jeff.

I saw Linda striding toward us.

"Well, I guess we'll have to ask her," I said.

"Ask me what?" Linda said from behind Jeff.

She looked at each of us with a quizzical look on her face. Still dressed in her dusty bike leathers, Linda waited for an answer. I quickly laid out the situation.

"Well," she teased, "if you're prepared to accept me into your family, then I think it's only right I pull my weight." She smiled. "Absolutely, I'll be glad to be a scout."

I was never in doubt.

"Thanks for that," I said as Linda and I made our way to my flat.

"It's the least I can do," she said. "We're family now."

I led the way into my flat, stepping over various bits of debris; glass crunched underfoot.

"I like what you've done to the place," Linda said, observing the carnage.

I scoffed. "Compliments of the late Derek Kaminsky. I don't know what he was after, but he sure wrecked the place looking for it."

"Sally told me what happened, about your friend, Tina."

I felt a pang in my heart.

"It shouldn't have happened. That's what's so galling. If I had been here..."

I couldn't get that thought out of my head.

"You don't know that," Linda said firmly. "I didn't know the guy, and by the sounds of it, I'm glad I didn't, but it was probably only a matter of time before Kaminsky tried something, whether you were here or not. You can't blame yourself. What's done is done."

I laughed bitterly. "You're the second person to tell me that today."

"Then you should listen."

I began gathering pieces of clothing, shaking them out and folding them into my backpack. I could feel Linda's eyes on me as I worked.

"I looked for you," I said. "Just after the after the evacuation started." I wasn't sure that she heard me.

"Oh?" she said quietly.

"Yeah, I went to your house on Stack Road."

"How did you know it was my house?"

"It was empty, and there was a Mini parked on the drive." I took the red scarf from one of the backpack's side pockets and threw it to Linda. "I found this in the hall."

"I thought I had lost this," she said.

"So ... what happened?" I asked.

"Long story, too long to go into now. Suffice to say, I had barely gotten to the house when the area was crawling with army personnel forcing everyone to evacuate. I ended up in London, Hyde Park, or what was left of it. The park had been burned, every tree and bush. I stayed for a while, but the place was a shambles, no hierarchy, no governing infrastructure, just chaos. I left and made my way to Ireland, intending to find Rob." She laughed. "Saying it like that makes it sound simple; it wasn't."

I continued to pack clothes, not looking at her as she leaned against the bedroom door frame. "Did you find him?"

"Not exactly..."

I met her gaze.

"Weeks later, I found his traction engine just outside of Dublin. The cab was on its side in a ditch; the interior was covered in blood." A cloud passed over Linda's face. "I made enquiries, but the so-called authorities had more pressing business. Eventually, I accepted the obvious."

"I'm sorry."

"Yeah…" she said.

"You're different," I said after a pause. "I don't just mean the hair and the leathers… different."

Linda cocked an eyebrow at me. "For better or worse?"

"Just different. More confident, sure of yourself. It suits you."

"That's what ten months of roaming about in the wilds of England and Ireland will do for you."

"But you're still not going to tell me what you were doing all that time, are you?"

"I will, Adam, just not now." She pushed away from the door jamb. "Come on, finish up. People are waiting on us."

I slung my backpack over my shoulder and headed for the door as Linda held it open. I could smell her perfume, Jasmine. As I paused in front of her, our eyes met, and before I knew what I was doing, I leaned in and kissed her. It wasn't planned. I didn't think about it. I just did it. There was momentary surprise as she stepped back from me, then she pulled me in and kissed me back, holding me close.

"About time," she whispered in my ear.

Suddenly grinning, she stepped away, all business again.

"Come on, time's wasting."

The courtyard was still buzzing. The kid's excited cries echoed around the enclosed space.

They gathered in the far corner by the chicken coop, which was now empty since all the chickens were slaughtered and eaten—another of Derek Kandinsky's evils. The children were under the watchful eye of Trish Morgan while the final preparations were made. I nodded to her as I passed, heading for Sally's.

"I'm going to check out my bike," Linda said. "Catch you later."

"Yeah, I'm going to call everyone together for a final briefing in about half an hour. I'll see you there."

She winked at me and loped off. I watched her departure, quietly enjoying the confident stride, her ready smile, and the toss of her head, held high as she greeted some of the others as she passed. This was a Linda I hadn't seen before.

Sally exited her flat just as I approached. She looked troubled, her normally cheerful expression creased, her bright red hair scrubbed back from her face.

"I was just coming to find you," she said.

"How are the patients?"

Sally pulled the front door shut, looking around to make sure no one was within earshot. "As well as can be expected. Peter hasn't woken up yet, but his vitals are good, and he's resting easy. It's Tina I'm worried about. She won't eat, won't drink, and getting her to take medication is a battle itself."

"Have the twins seen her?" I asked.

"Yeah. I kept the room dark and the blankets pulled up to her chin, making sure her face was mostly in shadow, so the little ones wouldn't be alarmed. They obviously knew their mum wasn't well, and they were upset, but seeing her made all the difference."

I sighed heavily. "Damn. Can I see her?"

"Of course, but not for long. I don't want to tire her any more than necessary. And I need to talk to you afterward."

As Sally had said, the room was dark, the double bed was pushed back against the far wall, and a dark mound rumpled the blankets. A single bed nestled against the nearer wall, and the light from the hallway fell across Peter Hogan's face which was turned to the wall, framed by his long, light brown hair.

Tina lay in the middle of the double bed. The bedside lamp was angled, so most of her face was in shadow, but the horrific injuries and swelling were still discernible in the low light. I felt my chest tighten. Carefully, I sat on the edge of the bed.

"Tina?" I said softly.

She stirred on the pillow, turning to look at me with one good eye; the other eye was closed, hidden beneath the purple and black bruising which covered the right side of her face. Sally had braided her long sandy hair, and it lay over the pillow.

Tenderly, I touched her hand. Tina pulled it quickly away.

"I'm not sorry," she said through mashed lips, giving her voice a slurred lisp.

"What?" I asked, puzzled.

"I'm not sorry. He's dead, and I'm glad..."

"Tina, you have nothing to be sorry for."

Her single brown eye blazed. "I'm not sorry." A solitary tear slipped down her cheek as she turned away.

Charlie and I had found Tina after we routed Kaminsky and his thugs for their attempt to take over the Block. She had been tied to her bed, naked, beaten, tortured cruelly ... raped. I tried repeatedly to drive the image of her lying helpless and used from my mind but couldn't.

I could still hear the gunshots echoing around the courtyard, the screams as people dove for cover as Tina kept firing the Smith and Wesson she had snatched from Charlie's holster. She walked toward her abuser, howling like a demented she-wolf, the firelight glowing off her naked body, revealing the horrific injuries inflicted on her sweat-sheened flesh—the cigarette burns, the welts, the bruises. Derek Kaminsky's body jerked like a manic marionette as bullet after bullet tore into him, ripping the life out of him. Even as he lay dead, the gun, now empty, clicked and clicked until I gently took it from her convulsing hands. Tina fled inside herself and locked herself away in a shattered mind where no one could reach her.

I watched her as she lay silently in her bed, wishing I could bring her out of the dark void in which she was lost. But I didn't know how.

In the other bed, Peter Hogan stirred. I looked over just as his eyes flickered open. Confusion clouded his face, making him wince. Reluctant to leave Tina, I quietly went over to him.

"Where... where am I?" he croaked.

"Relax. You're safe now. How do you feel?"

"Like I've been run over by a train."

"Close enough." I smiled thinly. "Do you remember anything?"

Peter's bruised and battered face worked as he searched his memory. "Kaminsky..." he mumbled.

"Yeah," I said. "Forget him. He's ... gone."

"I tried to stop him when he started to hurt that woman. I didn't know..." He blinked rapidly, remembering. "I stood between Kaminsky and the woman, told him to back off. Someone hit from behind. That's all I remember."

"You were badly beaten. You were lucky they stopped when they did."

"What about the woman? What happened to her?"

I glanced over to Tina. Peter looked too.

"Oh shit," he said. "I'm so sorry."

"It happened," I said grimly. "Now we have to put it behind us. Listen to Sally, get back on your feet, and we'll make everything come right, okay?"

He nodded, grunting with the small effort. I got up to go.

"Wait, " he said, "my bike...?"

I smiled. "It's in good hands. It's coming with us. The quicker you get out of this bed, the quicker you can ride again."

Sally was waiting outside the bedroom door.

"He's awake," I said. "He probably needs water."

She nodded. I looked at her askance, a disapproving look on my face.

"That was some crazy stuff you pulled this morning," I said. "You could have been seriously hurt. *'Shoot the prick!'* Really?"

More images of the dawn's confrontation with Kaminsky filled my mind: the wicked looking knife he held to Sally's throat, his gloating, and Sally's defiant refusal to be intimidated as the tableau played out in the Block's courtyard.

"Shoot him, Adam! Shoot the prick!" she had said—such words coming from a genteel woman's mouth.

"I would have shot him myself if I'd had a gun," Sally said hotly, "even before I'd seen what the bastard had done to Tina."

I hugged her. "You're one crazy woman, Sally Lowell!" I said, kissing her head.

She hugged me back. "I think we've all gone a little crazy," she replied.

"What did you want to talk to me about?" I asked.

"Oh, yes," she said. "Roger and some of the boys took the three rear seats out of the back of the coach. A load of canned food has been stacked there and made secure. They put boards on top and fixed two mattresses to use as beds for these two while we're travelling. Julie put up some curtains and soaped out the windows."

"What do you need from me?" I asked.

"I'm going to move the two of them in a few minutes, and I don't want the children to see them until we've got them set up in the coach."

"Leave it to me," I said. "I'll sort it out."

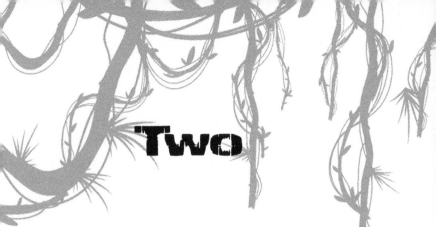

Two

Trish still had the children gathered over by the chicken coop, all seated in a half-moon around her on various boxes, chairs, and benches.

"Okay, so who knows the colours of the rainbow?" Trish asked

A forest of hands shot into the air, accompanied by eager cries of, "Me, me, me!"

"They have to be in the correct order."

The hands remained up.

"Alright, so how do we remember the correct order?"

The hands waved frantically.

"Susie?"

"Roy. G. Biv." Susie Yarrow beamed.

"That's right," Trish said. "And the colours are? Wei?"

Wei Lin, whose long hair was as black as coal, felt it necessary to stand up to give her answer. "Red, orange, yellow, green, blue..." she faltered.

"Indigo, violet!" Bobby Gray chimed in triumphantly.

"Very good. Well done, both of you!" Trish applauded.

I leaned in and quietly whispered in Trish's ear. She nodded.

"Okay children, now we're going to play another game. This one is called mind painting."

Trish quieted the ripple of excited voices.

"We've been talking about rainbows and clouds and the clear blue skies," Trish began. "Now, I want you all to close your eyes and think of all these things in one picture inside your head. Alright, everyone close your eyes, including you too, Chloe…"

I nodded over to Sally who was waiting by her front door. Tina was quickly carried out of the flat on a stretcher with a light sheet over her face as they hurried toward the coach.

"Imagine a big bright blue sky," Trish continued. "Put in some clouds, as big and fluffy as you like, then add the rainbow."

"Can we have more than one rainbow?" asked one of the children.

"You can have as many as you like, Laura," said Trish. "What else can you think of to put in the picture?"

"Birds!" said Bobby. "Great big eagles!"

"Okay," Trish said, smiling. "What else?"

"Airplanes!" David Donovan said.

"Put them in," Trish said. "Anything else?"

"Winged horses," said Susie.

"It's getting pretty crowded in the sky, don't you think?" Trish said. "Make sure they don't bump into each other."

Peter was just being carried onto the coach. Sally stood by the door of the bus. She nodded once her two patients were safely inside.

"Thanks," I said to Trish. "You can start loading the children onto the bus in a few minutes."

The group suddenly leapt to their feet; cheers and yells of "Yay!" filled the air.

I laughed at their excited innocence. *Oh, to be young again...*

The loading was going well, but it was taking too long. It was past noon, and we still had a lot to do. The children were all on the coach, watching a DVD under the supervision of Trish and Joan since they were not needed at the meeting I had called in Jules' flat. All the other adults attended. Everyone looked to me with an air of expectancy—not a feeling I relished. Old feelings rose inside me—the realisation that these people, my friends, my family, were all counting on me. Nagging doubt gnawed at me constantly; the responsibility weighed heavily.

"I'll make it brief," I said, dismissing the feeling. "We need to get moving. We go out in convoy. First Linda and Roger on the motorbikes, then me in the taxi, followed by Alan in the first transit. Charlie will take first shift driving the coach. The two bigger vans, driven by Jeff and Natalie, will bring up the rear. Everyone okay with this?"

There were murmurs of assent.

"Most of us can drive, and over time, we will teach the non-drivers. Meanwhile, we'll drive the vehicles in rotation to give everyone a break."

I opened the cardboard box on the table before me.

"Roger rigged up the transmitter given to us by Captain Williams in the coach. We have six handsets; each of the drivers and the motorbikes get one. The radios are to stay with the vehicles."

Charlie and Julie distributed the radios.

"One last thing: I want as many people as possible to be armed."

"Armed?" queried Sally. "What do we know about guns?"

"I realise that most of you have never had experience with guns. Why would you? But those of you who are willing can learn."

"Why do we need guns?" Teresa asked.

"Because Creeps aren't the only danger we may come across, as we have already seen. There might be others out there like Kaminsky and his cronies. We need to be able to defend ourselves," I answered. "It's not mandatory. Only those who are comfortable with the idea need carry a gun, but I don't need to point out that the more of us who are armed, the safer we will be."

"It makes sense, people," Charlie chimed in. "I didn't like the idea at first," he said, patting the holstered Smith and Wesson revolver on his hip. "But when it comes to my family…" He left the sentence unfinished.

"Several of us are already armed, but we can't be everywhere. I'll leave you to make up your own minds. If you think you can handle it, then come and see me or Jules, and we'll sort you out."

I was pleased to see Jules come forward and take one of the holstered Glock Seventeens from the box. Whether he was capable of using it, I had no idea, but that wasn't what it was about; Jules was a great believer in leading by example. He strapped the belt about his waist, adjusting the holster to a comfortable position.

Terry Moore stepped up. "I've never used one," he said.

"We'll teach you," Nat said, "and I'll show you how to use a bow if you like."

Terry grinned; the thought of being a Robin Hood obviously appealed to him. Tom and Andrew Taylor also took a Glock, though Tom refused to allow his other two sons, Paul and Stephen, to have one until they gained a little more experience. I secretly thought that wouldn't take long.

"Okay," Jules said, clapping his hands for attention. "We need to get going. Everyone know their assignments?"

There came a chorus of affirmations.

"Then let's get this show on the road."

The conversations became more animated as they all filed out of the flat. Linda and I brought up the rear.

"You okay?" she asked as we went out into the courtyard.

"I guess," I said, not wanting to give voice to my misgivings.

"You don't sound too sure."

"It's been a long few days." I looked at her. "I'm glad you're here though."

"Just as well," she said, grinning, "because you're stuck with me now."

The courtyard filled with the roar of engines as the vehicles passed through the archway for the last time. As we walked over to Linda's motorbike, Natalie was waiting for us.

"You ready for this?" she asked, dressed in black, a bow and a quiver of arrows across her back, and a Glock at her waist. It was obvious that she was more than ready.

"Absolutely," I said. I could tell that she had something on her mind.

"I was thinking..." she began hesitantly.

"That could be dangerous," I joked.

"Funny man," she said, making a face. "Seriously, I've been thinking about Kaminsky's men. They might come back here."

"And they're welcome to it. We've got all we need," I answered.

"That's not my point," Nat said. "I didn't want to say anything at the meeting in case of upsetting people."

"What are you talking about?" I queried, not liking the way the conversation was going.

"Look, Adam, I know they were bastards, and I'll never forgive them for what they did to Tina, but Kaminsky was the ringleader, and he's dead."

"Spit it out, Nat," I said.

"They're out there someplace, probably watching as we leave. As soon as we do, they'll come back. But they don't know about Operation Inferno."

"Are you saying that you want to find them and warn them?" I asked incredulously.

"No, I wouldn't even if we had time. I want to leave this, give them the chance to get out." Nat turned the board she was holding and showed me the message scrawled in red paint.

In four days, London will be firebombed. Take what you need and get out fast. This is NOT a joke. LEAVE ASAP!

I stared back at her. Honestly, I didn't know what to think or feel. I kept seeing Tina—the cigarette burns all over her body, the bruises, the knife cuts, all the physical abuse Kaminsky put her through. *Do I want to help the animals who did that?* I exchanged glances with Linda, who remained stoically non-committed. It was true what Nat said, it had all been Kaminsky, but that didn't excuse his men. They stood by and let it happen. In my eyes, they were just as guilty.

All the same, Nat had a point.

"Wait until everyone leaves," I said begrudgingly, fighting the conflicting emotions inside me. "I suggest propping it up beneath the arch, so they can't fail to see it. Don't hang about, Nat, and you can never tell anyone about this, alright?"

"I'll do it," Linda interjected. "If Nat doesn't drive the van, she'll be missed, but I can easily catch up on the bike."

Nat hesitated, uncertain.

"It's okay," I said. "Go."

"Thanks, thanks both of you," Nat said and hurried to her assigned van.

We watched as the coach pulled off, followed by the two transits.

"You've got a knack for doing the right thing at the right time," I said to Linda.

"I know you're not happy, but you were already thinking of doing something like this yourself," Linda said. "You'd better get a move on, or you'll be missed too. Tell Roger I'll catch up."

Until she said it, I didn't realise that Linda was right.

Smiling, I headed for the cab, then stopped and went back to kiss her. To feel her arms around me and kissing me back made my heart race.

"You be careful out there; don't do anything crazy," I said.

She looked at me with wide-eyed innocence. "Who? Me?"

I drove out of the arch. Horns blared as I took up position at the front of the convoy. Children waved from the coach windows. Pulling up beside Roger, I wound down my window.

"Linda will catch up, Roger!"

He nodded, flipped down the visor of his crash helmet, revved the bike, and led us off.

Minutes later, Linda blasted past me. A quick wave of her hand and a flash of her red scarf streaming behind her, and she was gone, racing after Roger, who was already out of sight. The going was easy, but we knew that. Alan and Jeff had scouted the first part of the journey days ago: East to the A2, south to the M25 Orbital, on to the Dartford Tunnel.

"Is the tunnel a good idea?" Jules had asked a few hours before as we sat in the courtyard whilst work was being finished on the coach.

"I've no intention of going through the tunnel," I said. *"We've no idea what we'll find in there; it's too big a risk. Blockage, flooding, who knows what? If we can't get through, it would be a bitch getting back out."*

"We could scout it first," Charlie suggested.

"No, I'm not sending motorbikes in there unprotected. We'll go over the bridge, keep in the

open. Then we'll follow the north side of the M25 around to the North Corridor and on to the M1."

"Seems like a good plan," Jules agreed.

"It's got to be," I said. "It's all we've got."

Those words came back to me as we drove toward the A2. I could see Alan in the small transit, fifty-odd yards behind me; the coach was behind him. I sighed heavily. I couldn't help but think I should have gone camping when I had the chance...

The A2 was pretty clear with only the occasional abandoned car. The undergrowth on either side of the motorway was thick but not enough to intrude on the road. I wondered how long this would be the case. I kept seeing movement in the undergrowth but was unable to determine if it was the wind or something more sinister.

"Adam, d'you copy?"

"Go ahead, Linda," I returned.

"We're at the M25 exit. There's a few cars blocking the access road; we're going to try and move them."

"Copy that. We're about fifteen minutes out."

I saw the motorbikes parked at the foot of the off ramp. I pulled up beside them and got out of the cab just in time to see a red Toyota disappear over the embankment, bouncing over the grass as it careened out of sight. The heat hit me like a sledgehammer; the climate was definitely changing. England had never known such temperatures. Another car rolled down the ramp—a dark green Ford. It joined the Toyota in the neighbouring field. The sound of crunching metal and breaking glass split the air as they collided. Roger and Linda appeared at the top of the incline.

"Oh, you get here when all the work's done!" Linda jibed, walking down the ramp toward me.

"You're too fast for your own good, girlie!" I returned.

"It's clear now," Roger said, wiping the sweat off his forehead. "I can't see any immediate problems ahead."

"We'll go on to make sure," Linda said, taking her crash helmet from the motorbike's pillion. She came up to me and gave me a quick kiss before plonking it on her head. "Try and keep up," she grinned, mounting her bike.

With a wave of her hand, she roared up the exit ramp with Roger close behind. Dripping sweat, I returned to the cab just as the convoy was approaching.

"Everything okay?" Charlie's voice came over the radio.

"All good, mate," I said into the mike. "Keep it rolling."

I allowed Alan to pass me, followed by the other vehicles. Once on the M25, I took up my position in the lead.

"Well, that's a bummer," Charlie said, looking at the mass of cars blocking the motorway. "How do we get past that lot?"

There must have been nearly a thousand cars, vans, and lorries jammed in front of the tunnel entrances, spreading out across the wide access roads and blocking our approach to the Queen Elizabeth the Second Bridge.

"We're going to have to move them," I said.

"What?" asked Charlie's wife, Julie, incredulously. "How? Where are we going to move them to?"

"There are fewer cars on the right," Nat said. "Isn't that the way we need to go?"

"Yeah," I said, looking in the direction she was pointing. I had to squint my eyes against the glare despite the sunglasses I was wearing. "We need to head north using the southbound carriageway."

Heat shimmered over the myriad vehicles, a multi-coloured rainbow cauldron.

"I knew there would be cars," I said, "just not this bad."

"You knew?" Charlie asked, a little irritation edging his voice. "Then why the hell would we come this way?"

"Because it's the best way, the only way," I said. "You saw the maps in Captain Williams command tent, the 'no-go' areas. Surrey was totally red, and it's three times the distance. East London was a definite nonstarter. We'd have to negotiate the Blackwall Tunnel, and I'm betting the traffic problem is worse than here, with no alternative routes, just backtracking.

"Going through London would mean dealing with the military, and there's no way we could risk being detained. Even if they eventually let us through, it would cause too much delay. This was ... *is* our only option. Once we get across the bridge, our options will increase if time gets short. We can turn north onto the M11, the A10, or the A1, get clear of London, and then cut across country back to the M1."

"Well, I figure we've got about four hours of daylight," said Jules. "Standing here gassing isn't going to get it done."

"Look over there," Roger said. "There are less vehicles in those two lines, maybe forty cars. Let's start there."

"We'll keep the children occupied," Trish said, wiping her face with a handkerchief. "It's too hot to let them off the bus."

I nodded. "Terry!"

Terry Moore turned at my call.

"You got binoculars?"

"Yep!" he said, raising his backpack.

"Get on top of the coach, keep a look out, three hundred and sixty degrees, and put a hat on!"

Pulling a baseball cap out of his pack, Terry slapped it on his head and headed for the coach.

Two

Three

The heat was brutal. The metal of the cars was too hot to touch bare-handed, so we were forced to pull down sleeves or use T-shirts to avoid painful contact. We were all soaked in sweat and gasping in the humid air within minutes. Julie and some of the older children brought us water as slowly but surely, we cleared a path. Thankfully most of the vehicles still had their keys in the ignition. Though we tried, none of them started, but it made it easier to move them. The odd one or two that didn't have keys forced us to smash side windows, and moving them became a bitch when the steering locks kicked in.

Not having to worry where we dumped them was the only blessing. We just needed them to be clear and not causing an obstruction. We pushed them across the carriageway, rolled the cars down embankments, anywhere.

"We're losing daylight," Jules reminded us, his dark face glistening with sweat.

"I know," I said. "I was hoping to be well on the other side of the bridge by nightfall."

"There aren't many cars left; we can still make it," he said breathlessly.

"I think you've done enough. Go rest in the coach."

He glowered at me.

"No arguments."

With a grunt, he went off, unable to disguise the stiffness in his back as he limped along. He was sixty-three years old, pushing cars in the searing heat alongside the younger men, determined to pull his own weight. I only hoped I had his vigour and vitality when I got to his age.

"We should be able to get through now," Charlie said, nearly an hour later.

"Good," I said, looking at the lowering sky. The sun still had a little way to go before sunset. "Let's get across the bridge at least."

Terry was still on top of the coach along with Teresa Wright, who had produced a large blue and white golfing umbrella to use as shade. They were two of a kind: quiet, self-contained, and traumatised by their respective negative experiences with the black dust.

Teresa was older than Terry by about eight years, but it didn't seem to matter to them. After I had saved him from a group of Creeps that had him trapped in an industrial waste bin, Terry had gone inside himself and refused to speak. He wouldn't communicate; he just ate and slept. It was Teresa who brought him out of his shell. She sat with him and talked for nearly two days. We never found out what they talked about, and neither she nor Terry ever said. A bond had formed between them, and they were spending more and more time in each other's company. I, for one, was glad. They made a great couple—perfect for each other.

"Terry! We're ready to roll!" I called.

He waved, took down the umbrella, and they clambered down off the coach.

"How's Tina doing?" I asked as Sally entered the coach.

She paused on the steps. "She's healing, physically at least. She's eaten a little. I think it's the twins who are holding her together."

Mark and Matthew were Tina's six-year-old twins; she always called them her babies. They'd been fretting about their mother, and Trish, our resident teacher and nanny, was doing a great job comforting and assuring them that everything was going to be alright.

"Good," I said. "I'll see her later."

Teresa and Terry appeared from around the coach, both smiling. Terry's baseball cap was turned backward, the size adjuster across his forehead. He was definitely coming out of his shell because he obviously thought he looked cool.

"Good job, Sunshine," I said, clapping him on the shoulder as they entered the coach.

Terry's smile widened.

Back in the taxi, I thumbed the microphone. "Okay, let's move. Try keeping a little closer till we're over the bridge."

"We're already on the bridge," Linda came back. "There's a lot of vehicles up here. We're going to have to weave our way through, but Roger says it clears about halfway across. Other than that, I don't think there's any major obstacles."

"Good stuff. We're on our way."

Charlie eased the coach along the narrow lane, driving out onto the bridge approach. Alan had already gone ahead with the first transit. I followed the coach, and the other two transits brought up the rear.

The bridge, sometimes referred to as The Dartford Crossing, was an 812-yard-long cable-stayed bridge which carried the four south-bound lanes of the M25. The northbound lanes went through the tunnel situated just to the left of the bridge. It rose 137 yards above the River Thames, and on completion, it was Europe's largest cable-supported bridge with a total span of 450 yards.

Now, it was a vehicle graveyard.

The cars were dotted haphazardly across the first part of the bridge. Why they had been abandoned was anyone's guess. Weaving in and out, following Charlie's lead in the coach, we made slow progress.

"Adam, I think you need to see this," Roger said over the radio.

"What's the problem?" I said, my heart sinking.

"No problem as such," Roger said. "It's the vines."

Curiosity piqued, I continued until the coach brake lights brought me to a stop. Roger and Linda were on the left side of the bridge, looking down over the balustrade.

"What is it?" I asked as I approached.

"See for yourself." Linda nodded downward.

I looked.

"Oh shit..." I muttered.

The scene was a carbon copy of Thamesmead: huge vines, writhing and twisting at the water's edge, slowly choking the River Thames. Massive serpentine limbs entwined around the concrete pillars which supported the bridge, creeping upward, inch by inch. Leaning out, I tried to see how far the vines extended in their inexorable ascent. I couldn't.

"I checked the other side," Roger said. "It's the same. They're growing along the river's edge, masses of them, making their way inland."

Charlie and Natalie had joined us. Looking over the bridge, Charlie whistled in amazement.

"They keep on growing like that, they'll eventually bring the whole bridge down," he said wonderingly.

"I don't know about that," I said, "but they will cut off another escape route, going on the premise that the bridge survives Operation Inferno. We'd better move. I don't think it's a good idea to stay here too long."

"I think it's already too late," said Roger. "Look!"

Shapes were moving among the vines, moving fast, making their way up the writhing tentacles toward us with almost supernatural ease.

"Creeps and they've seen us," Linda gasped.

"Back to the coach. Go! Go!" I ordered.

With a screech of tires, Linda and Roger took their place in front of the coach as Charlie hurried into the driver's seat. With a cloud of exhaust fumes, Charlie revved the idling engine, slipped into gear, and followed the bikes.

A movement to my left made me turn as I ran for the cab. Four Creeps were already on the bridge, bounding over the cars toward me. Drawing the Glock, I let loose five quick shots and was pleased to see two of the brutes go down; the other two ducked for cover. I ran like hell.

I sensed, rather than saw, another Creep behind me, hurtling over the balustrade. Before I had time to turn and face it, it barrelled into me, knocking me off my feet. I bounced off the bonnet of a car, hitting the ground rolling and barely managing to hold onto the gun. I scrambled to my feet, desperately searching for my attacker.

The buckling car roof behind me sounded like a clap of thunder as the Creep landed heavily, looming above me in silent rage. I whirled around, gaping in shock at the monster—hoary arms held wide, jaws agape and dribbling saliva, feral eyes glaring down at me. It was huge, at least five feet tall, and a dark streak of fur raked across its chest like a lightning bolt, black against the white.

Raising the gun, I took quick aim, but as quick as I was, the beast was faster. Its claw lashed out, and the Glock spun from my hand as I staggered back. The Creep's leaping body blotted out the sky. Desperately, I threw myself aside, drawing my heavy hunting knife as I turned to face the monster.

Less than eight feet separated us on the ground. I felt dwarfed by the creature. Even though I was taller, it easily outweighed me by fifty pounds of sheer muscle. Fast as a striking snake, it lashed out at me. I was barely able to sidestep the ferocious blow. The car door crumpled as the three-inch claws struck it, gouging the bright metal. The side window shattered with a dull popping sound, and glass cascaded like a shower of ice.

Without pause, the beast struck back as I slashed with my knife. There was a brief moment of resistance as the razor-sharp blade sliced through the Creep's wrist. The severed claw flew through the air in a gout of brackish blood.

Grabbing its wrist as it poured blood, the brute glared at me. Total madness blazed in those demonic eyes, turning my blood cold. I knew I wouldn't survive another attack. Raising its arms and turning its bestial face to the darkening sky, the monster silently howled—only it wasn't silent.

I grunted as my head filled with its dreadful screams; my brain felt like it was going to explode. Through watering eyes, I saw the Creep tense, preparing to charge. I wanted to bring up my knife in a last-ditch effort to defend myself, but my arms wouldn't respond. The cacophony of the weird scream still reverberated through my whirling mind. In my mind's eye, I saw my death, torn to red ruin by the claw and fang as the Creep tore into me.

Something whizzed past my ear. The Creep staggered, gaping in surprise at the arrow protruding from its right shoulder. I turned just as Nat nocked a second arrow to her bow and took aim. With absolute disdain, the Creep tore the arrow from its shoulder and threw it at us. Blood gushed from the terrible wound as Nat drew back her bowstring again. The creature just stepped back, its hip striking the railing of the bridge, and in one fluid movement, rolled over the balustrade and dropped out of sight.

"Run!" Nat screamed.

Shifting her aim, Nat put the arrow through another Creep's throat, and it dropped stone dead. Then she raced after me toward the cab. I pulled open the rear door as I fell into the driver's seat. Nat hurtled into the rear of the cab.

"Go! Go! Go!"

It seemed like a good idea, so I got out of there as fast as I could.

Four

"Adam? Adam?" Jules' concerned voice barked from the speaker.

With an effort, I shook the cobwebs out of my head. I was in shock, driving by sheer instinct, weaving through abandoned vehicles until we were suddenly clear, and I put my foot down.

"Adam, answer me, goddammit!" Jules demanded.

I grabbed the mike and croaked, "Yeah Jules, I'm here."

"Thank God! You had us worried. Is Nat with you?"

I glanced behind; Nat was staring out the rear window.

"Yeah, yeah, we're both here. We're okay."

"Adam, tell them to keep moving," Nat said through the dividing window which separated the rear of the cab from the front. "The Creeps are using the bridge's superstructure, dozens of them, and they're coming fast."

Glancing in the side mirror, I could see dark shapes flitting through the cables, leaping from one to the other. More Creeps were scuttling along the topmost cables strung between the two massive support towers. Even more lumbered along the road in an ape-like gate, all feet and knuckles.

"Shit," I swore, opening the mike. "Everybody keep going. Get as far away from here as you can. The bastards are coming after us."

"Okay, will do. D'you need help?"

"No. Get going," I said tersely, throwing the mike into the passenger well and sticking the pedal to the metal.

The convoy soon came into sight, barrelling along the motorway. Linda and Roger were continually circling, acting as a rear guard.

"They've stopped," Nat said. "They're squatting on the bridge and cables, watching us."

"Thank Christ for that," I said, easing up on the gas.

Three miles later, the convoy came to a stop. I pulled up beside the coach, and Roger and Linda appeared on either side of the cab. Nat got out and was immediately surround by Jules, Sally, Charlie, and the others. With a heavy sigh, I followed her. It had been close, too close.

"What the hell was that all about? How'd they get on us so quickly?" Jules asked.

I was at a loss for words as I looked back along the motorway. Terry was already climbing up on top of the coach, his binoculars at the ready.

"They knew we were there," I said. "They heard our engines."

"Shit, they were fast," Charlie said.

"You look a little shaken. You okay?" asked Sally.

I brushed the question off but looked at Nat.

"Thanks," I said.

"Seems saving your arse is becoming a habit," she said, conspicuously brandishing her bow.

"I'll never let anyone make fun of your bow again, I promise," I said wanly.

"Was it my imagination or was the Creep that attacked you bigger?" Charlie asked. "I saw it in the rear-view, and I thought it was magnified."

"It wasn't the mirror," I said. "They're getting bigger."

"The others didn't look any bigger," Nat replied.

Thinking about it, I realised she was right.

"They must have been waiting for us under the bridge," said Jules. "Talk about *The Three Billy Goats Gruff.*"

"Did you hear it?" I asked, turning to Nat. "The big Creep, did you hear it scream?"

Nat looked puzzled. "No, I got the same weird silence as always. It never ceases to freak me out."

"It screamed," I said. "I heard it, or at least I think I heard it. It was in my head, filling my mind, harsh, brutal..."

"In your head?" Charlie asked. "Jesus!"

"I never heard a thing," Nat said.

"Captain Williams said they thought the Creeps communicated via some sort of telepathy or maybe an ultrasonic frequency too high for the human ear," Charlie said. "Could that be it?"

"I don't know." I couldn't help but shudder. "But I don't want to feel it again. It made my skin crawl."

"We're going to have to discuss it later," Jules said. "I don't feel safe here; we need to move." His eyes continually scanned back down the motorway, as if expecting to see a horde of Creeps lumbering after us.

I could still feel the Creep in my head. I felt violated. The hairs on my arms tingled with electric dread. It was like some sort of mental vampire sucking at my mind. *What are these things? Where did they come from?* I was beginning to wonder if we would ever find the means to get rid of them, once and for all. The alternative was too horrible to contemplate.

"Adam, are you okay?" Jules shook my shoulder. "You weren't with us for a minute there."

I smiled weakly. "Just a little shaken up still."

I looked around, taking my bearings, then nodded up the road.

"There's a wide space about three miles farther on. We can stop there for the night," I said.

"Shouldn't we just keep going?" Charlie asked. "We could take over for each other, drive through the night."

"It's too dangerous. We need to see what's in front of us, and it would put Roger and Linda at risk. We'll stop, set up a perimeter, rest for the night, and move on at first light."

Nat thanked Andrew Taylor who had driven the van when she saw I was in trouble, then she took over the driving again.

Charlie pulled the coach off the motorway, parking at an angle to a high wire mesh fence. The other vehicles formed a crude half-circle around it, giving us some protection. How effective it would be against the Creeps was questionable, but we worked with what we had.

Jules worked out a quick rota for guard duty, starting with Terry and Nat. Teresa accompanied Terry on top of the coach, and it was obvious from his happy expression that he was relishing his newfound responsibilities. Nat took up position on one of the vans. I let them know that they would be relieved in three hours by Alan and Jeff.

Meanwhile, Sally, with the help of the Taylor boys, hauled out a cut oil drum from the storage bay on the coach. It was packed with logs and charcoal, which they dumped out in order to build a cooking fire in the drum, using a wire mesh to cook on. It wasn't long before a ruddy glow lit up our little encampment, and the smell of beef stew filled the air.

I wondered if this was what it had been like in the early days of the American west when the settlers crawled across the deserts of the New World in covered wagons, searching for a place to settle. Without a doubt, there were definite similarities: the lack of resources, the danger of hostile attacks, the uncertainty of what tomorrow might bring.

"You should eat," Linda said, handing me a plate.

I had been sitting on a box by the cab a little away from the main group. I didn't want them to see that I was still a little shaken up.

"Thanks, not sure if I can though," I said, accepting the meal.

"We've got a long journey ahead of us; you need to eat," she insisted, forcing the hunk of bread into my hand and sitting on the box beside me.

"Yes ma'am," I said, and she elbowed me in the ribs.

Jeff appeared in front of me with a cloth bundle in his hand.

"Here," he said, handing me the bundle.

It was a Glock.

"Try not to lose this one," he said, turning away. "Oh, and it's loaded," he threw over his shoulder.

"Thanks Jeff," I said and immediately holstered the gun

The night sky was clear, filled with a million stars. The temperature hadn't dropped much, and I didn't think it would. Because of the heat, Trish, liaising with what parents there were, allowed the children to sit around the fire on blankets, eating and chatting happily. They were glad to get off the cramped bus for a while before bedding down safely back on the coach. Once again, I marvelled at the children's resilience, their ability to adjust to any given situation.

"So, finish telling me about Scotland," Linda said, snuggling up to me.

"It's beautiful," I said as I put my arm around her. "Or at least it was. I'm not so sure now. And it can be hard. I prefer the west highlands, the mountains, Applecross, Torridon."

"Are we going to be able to survive there?"

"Yeah, I think so, providing I'm right about the cold."

Still, that little doubt niggled at me. Because of its beauty, a lot of would-be hikers and campers frequently underestimated Scotland's weather, neglecting to note the rapidity in which conditions could change, literally from one hour to the next. They were also lulled by the terrain, which, while spectacular, was also harsh and unforgiving to the unwary. Continually damp and often cold with very little shelter, the more remote areas could be deadly for the unprepared. Totally unexpected storms could sweep in, wild and tumultuous—torrential rain, freezing wind, and blizzards in winter that rivalled Antarctica, inundating the glens and valleys with impassable drifts of snow.

Has Scotland changed? I didn't know. I could only hope, for all our sakes.

"We'll just have to take it one step at a time," Linda said. "We'll make it; you'll see."

I smiled and kissed the top of her head.

"One step at a time..." I murmured.

I waited until Sally had taken the twins back outside after visiting their mother before looking in on Tina. Sally told me that Tina had eaten some of the beef stew and was glad to see Matt and Mark but still refused to say more than a few words, mainly "thanks" and "no."

"Tina?" I sat down on the edge of the makeshift bed.

She continued to stare at the soaped window of the coach.

"How are you feeling?"

Slowly, her head turned. Her right eye was still swollen shut, the bruising livid. It was going to take a long time to fade.

"Thank you for looking after my babies," she whispered, the mashed lips still making her words slightly slurred.

"Mark and Matt are everybody's babies, all the kids are, but they still need their mum," I said gently. "They need you."

Tears welled in her eyes. One tracked a silver line down her bruised and battered left cheek. "He hurt me, Adam, really hurt me. He made me feel dirty, unclean. He said and did such vile things..."

My guts twisted up; sorrow and hate and shame roiled inside me all at once.

"No one will ever hurt you again, I promise," I said, reaching for her hand, but once again, she drew it away. "We're heading for a new life, Tina, a new beginning for all of us. We can leave all this behind. We're family now, brothers and sisters joined in a common cause to love and protect one another, and we will, always; that's what families do. You have to believe that. Hang on to it, if only for the sake of the twins."

She said nothing, turning her face back to the sightless window, withdrawing into her secret world. She looked so lost, so ... broken. I knew she heard me, but I wasn't sure she was taking it in. At that moment, even though I was a non-believer, I truly hoped that Derek Kaminsky was burning in Hell.

First light dawned. The night had passed without incident, and everyone was eager to be on our way. Terry was on top of the coach again, by himself this time, even though it was not his shift, scanning back along the motorway with his binoculars.

Linda handed me a cup of tea. I was never one for coffee first thing in the morning.

"Sleep well?" she asked, giving me a quick kiss on the lips.

"I guess. You?"

"Like a baby." She grinned.

"You alright out there on the bike?" I asked.

She laughed. "I've spent the last eight months 'out there on a bike.' It's not a problem."

"Just checking," I said, abashed. "Eight months?"

"The first two months, I went by *Shanks' Pony* or was in a car. And I am not the only one enjoying being on a motorcycle; I think Roger's loving it too," Linda remarked.

"Motorbikes are his passion," I said.

"And what's your passion?" Linda sidled closer, a twinkle in her eye.

"Behave," I said. "We've got an audience."

A bunch of kids were standing by the coach, watching and pointing at us, giggling and laughing. I leaned in and whispered in Linda's ear.

"Ask me later."

She finished her tea in a couple of quick swallows and got up. "Deal," she said and went to find Roger.

The day was already getting hot as the merciless sun rose in a clear, unforgiving sky. Everything was quickly packed away, and the children were bundled onto the bus after a quick breakfast of tea and toast cooked over the fire. The Taylor boys dumped out the ashes of the fire and loaded it back into the coach storage bay. Engines burst to life as Linda and Roger rode out of the enclave, heading north-west.

The convoy followed.

We kept to a steady forty miles an hour when we could, but the motorway was littered with more and more abandoned vehicles. A few of them had been involved in accidents, making it necessary to slow down and negotiate past the wrecks, being mindful of the debris and broken glass on the carriageway. We couldn't afford damaged or punctured tyres.

The passing landscape was alien on both sides of the motorway. Rows of empty houses stood silent; patches of sickly green and black crept across the roofs. Vines overran every garden and open space, but they weren't so big here, and I assumed it was due to having less water. Thankfully, there weren't many trees. It was obvious that the Creeps were arboreal, preferring woods and forests to open spaces. I'd discussed this with Alan and Jeff as well as Linda, seeing as we had the most experience of the "outside," and they agreed. No trees meant no Creeps, or at least it meant less Creeps, which could only be good for us.

I fretted a little about Scotland, forever keeping it to myself. *What if this weather change has affected Scotland? What if it is no longer cold enough there? What if I am wrong about the cold in the first place? Maybe the vines and Creeps have already infested the Highlands…?*

It didn't bear thinking about. I shrugged the thoughts away. *What did Linda say? "One step at a time."*

Every time we encountered the Creeps, there was something different. They had started out small, like cats. Then they grew larger and began to use weapons, forming organised and concerted attacks. Now ... the memory of that scream in my head made me shudder. A disconcerting thought rose like an insidious worm. It was ridiculous, stupid, but it wouldn't stop going around in my mind. *What if the Creeps are developing psychic abilities? What if high frequency sound isn't their means of communication?*

"No," I said out loud. "Now I'm being paranoid!"

"Adam, d'you copy?"

I was glad when Linda's voice startled me out of my morbid ruminations. I opened the mike.

"Yeah, Linda?"

"You need to stop the convoy at the next exit and get up here."

"What's wrong?" I asked, the now familiar feeling of my heart sinking once more washed over me.

"It looks like we're going to have to find another way north..." she said.

Five

The blockade of cars soon came into view, sunlight glinting on chrome and glass. Linda was standing on top of a pile of pallets loaded onto the flatbed of an articulated lorry. It was an effort to climb up the wooden mountain in the oppressive heat and join her.

"I can't see where it ends," Linda said, handing me a pair of binoculars. "The road bends to the right, and it's a mass of cars from here till it goes out of sight."

From our vantage point, we had a pretty good view of the situation.

"We're not going to be able to move them this time," I said, peering through the glasses. "The wall on the left means dragging every vehicle backward to clear it. We haven't the time."

"So, what do we do?" she asked.

"I don't know," I said honestly.

The motorway was basically enclosed by a wall on the left and a concrete meridian topped with a heavy mesh fencing on the right, starting about fifty yards farther on. Immediately to our right was the standard rail, separating the north and south bound carriageways. There was no embankment to push the cars down, no open area to get them out of the way. The heat coming off the massed metal took my breath away; I was totally sheathed in sweat.

"Where's Roger?" I asked.

"The central railing has been removed by some enterprising motorist, obviously attempting to bypass this lot. Roger went to see if it offered any options."

Almost on cue, Linda's radio crackled.

"Lin, y'there?"

"Yeah, Roger. Any luck?"

"None and sod all," he said glumly. "Whoever came this way didn't get far. It's clear for about a mile and a half, then they ran headlong into oncoming traffic, literally. There's one hell of a fender bender up here; it's hard to tell how many vehicles were involved. There was a fire, lots of burnt shells, no tyres, so there's no way to move the debris even if we wanted too."

"Shit," Linda said. "Okay, Roger, you better get back here."

"Bollocks," I muttered, echoing Linda's sentiment.

"What now?" she asked.

"I'm not sure," I said, raking wet strands of hair off my face.

"Do you know where we are?"

"Yeah, just north of Romford. Thing is, I only know the main roads in this area, I've no idea about the back streets."

"So, we get onto a main road," Linda said simply.

"Easier said than done. This section of the M25 hasn't got a lot of exits, and I stopped the convoy where it was. If this jam had just been a few miles farther on, we could have taken the M11 and gone north," I said, clucking my tongue in frustration.

"Is there an alternative?"

I looked back the way we came and thought about it. Sweat irritated my face and trickled uncomfortably down my back. "We need to get out of this heat; I can't think straight," I said and started to climb down off the pallets.

Roger came roaring up on his motorcycle. Dismounting, he pulled off his helmet and scrubbed at his hair.

"Looks like we're going nowhere fast," he said.

"Any ideas?" I asked.

"The A12 goes north; we passed it a little way back," Roger said.

I tried to remember Captain Williams' map which showed the concentration of vines in various areas. I remembered East London was bad, but I couldn't recall how far east and north the vines extended.

"I think the A12 is our best option," I said slowly. "But not north; there's too much green, especially around Epping Forest. We'll drop down and pick up the A406. It runs almost parallel with the M25, but I'm afraid that means a lot more riding back and forth to check our route for you and Linda. We need to get back up onto the M25 as soon as possible."

"Not a problem." Linda shrugged. "Roger?"

"Whatever we need to do," he agreed.

"Let's get back to the others," I said. "Let them know what's happening."

I'd travelled the M25 dozens of times. The northeast section was one of those drive-straight-through areas, a means to an end. There were few exits and even less to see—no landmarks of note or real points of interest. Hence, I didn't know the area very well. I cursed silently to myself. This was as bad as Thamesmead; what should have taken hours was stretching into days. Now, I was stuck here in the middle of nowhere and unsure of where to go, resorting to best-guess strategy; considering our present situation, that was not good either.

"So," asked Charlie, "not only have we got to go back, but you want us to go closer to the city?"

"I think it's our best option," I said.

"If getting fried to a crisp is one of those options, then I'd have to agree," Charlie said.

"Charlie!" Julie was horrified.

"No, Julie, he's right," I said. "I shouldn't make all the decisions, take all the responsibility. If someone sees something or thinks I'm wrong in any way, they need to speak up. Their dissent helps me; it makes me see things clearer. It might even make me see something I've missed or not thought of. So, if there's a better option, let's hear it."

Everyone looked blankly at each other.

"Why not go north on the A12?" Charlie asked.

"Because it's a small motorway, and the exits are miles apart. It gives us no alternatives. Plus, it passes close to Epping Forest, which makes it dangerous.

"If we pick up the A406, Linda and Roger can scout ahead and lead us to the quickest route back to the M25 and the North Corridor."

"So, it's more of a race than ever?" asked Jules.

I nodded.

"Then let's do it."

Everyone headed for their vehicles, but Charlie hung back.

"Adam, I don't mean to question you..."

"No, Charlie, I meant what I said: call me out anytime you think I'm making a mistake, always."

He suddenly gripped my hand and hugged me.

"I've got to tell you, I'm scared shitless," he whispered.

"Me too, mate," I said. "Me too."

And I was.

Finally, some luck! We backtracked to the A12, turned south to the A406, went west for about five miles, and then Linda called to report that the way on the M25 was clear. I heard the cheering over the mike as Charlie held it open; horns blasted and morale soared a thousand percent.

We still had fifty miles to go to the North Corridor.

Everyone has heard the old adage: Never tempt fate. Ten miles on, I thought that was exactly what we'd done. The going had been easy, we were eating up the miles, and I was thinking we would spend one more night camping and push on through the North Corridor the following day. I had no idea what exactly that would entail, though the military figured in my thinking. I was planning to use the evacuation

as our reason for heading north and hoped it wouldn't be a problem; tomorrow would tell. Dusk was a couple of hours away, but the sky was already darkening. I could feel pressure in my ears as if the sky was pushing down on me.

"Charlie, Adam, over to the west, can you see that?"

"I see it, Alan," I said. "I wish I didn't."

Dark clouds rolled in from the west at an alarming speed; huge writhing masses swept across the landscape like a behemoth on the eve of Armageddon. The ground beneath the tyres of the cab vibrated, and lightning flashed beneath the ebony canopy, leaping from cloud to cloud in dazzling bursts that left black spots dancing before my eyes, sticks of crackling energy ripping across the turbulent sky.

The first clap of thunder was monstrously loud; the force shook the entire cab, making the metal panels thrum and creak. The wind picked up, and pieces of paper and other detritus flew across the motorway like phantom bats in the failing light. If it became gale force, it would be a problem.

"Jesus!" I breathed.

The second clap of thunder was like a hammer of the gods, and the Earth was the anvil.

"Charlie, get to an underpass, take shelter. Linda, Roger, get back here! Everyone, follow Charlie!" I shouted into the mike.

Thankfully, a wide overpass loomed out of the gathering darkness half a mile ahead. We barely reached it when the heavens opened up. Charlie hauled the coach to a stop close to the edge of the motorway by the wall. I pulled up alongside him, my tyres screeching from braking too hard.

Alan came up behind me, and the other two vans, driven by Tom and Jeff, respectively, stopped behind Alan. Seconds later, the two bikes came roaring in, the pouring rain parted like a curtain as they skidded to a stop. Roger was nearly pitched from the bike as it slewed around on the wet ground.

I leapt out of the cab, watching the storm rage. The rain was loud in my ears, and the thunder boomed louder.

"Bloody hell!" Charlie said, coming to stand beside me. "A fucking year without rain and then we get this!"

"It's almost tropical," I said, sticking my hand out into the rain. "It's warm."

"Is it safe?" Julie called from the coach doorway.

"It's just a storm," I assured her.

"Yeah," she said drily, "I remember the last one."

"We could have done without this," Jules said, joining us. "It's practically nil visibility."

Linda removed her helmet and shook her head; her dusty leathers were now wet and shiny.

"Damned rain nearly had me over," she said.

"Me too," Roger said, looking at the skid marks his bike had left on the concrete upon entering the underpass. "Twice."

"D'you think it's going to last?" asked Charlie.

"Let's hope not," I said. "With a bit of luck, it will be like normal tropical storms, violent but brief."

"Adam, is it okay for some of the kids to get off the coach? They want to see the rain," asked Trish.

"Yeah, they should be alright. Just make sure none of them wander off. Maybe we can get something to eat till this lot blows over?"

"I'll sort it," Julie said.

"What if it doesn't ease up?" Charlie asked. "I don't fancy trying to drive through that lot."

"We may have to," I said grimly. "We can't stay here too long."

Julie, Joan, and Sally set up some tables from the coach's storage bay along with some cool boxes with the makings of sandwiches. Stephen Taylor attended to a butane gas stove and soon had some water on to boil.

It was like being in a cave beneath twin waterfalls. The raindrops were huge, splattering hard onto the concrete and leaping back up into the air over a foot. The thunder and lightning frightened some of the kids, who refused to leave the coach. The more adventurous relished the storm, sticking their hands into the torrential rain and laughing with delight as the warm water splashed over their fingers.

I laid a map of the United Kingdom across the bonnet of the cab and perused the way north. The obvious route was the M1 up to Leeds where it became the A1. We would turn there and head west along the M6 toward Manchester then north to Glasgow. I was a little concerned about passing through the Lake District, since it's very green and traditionally very wet. The vines must surely have taken hold there. I looked to the far north—Scotland

and the West Highlands. I tapped a finger on it as I explained the proposed route.

"It sounds easy when you put it like that," said Charlie, chomping into a sandwich.

"I think our main concern is getting past the North Corridor," Jules said. "Once we're away from London and out of danger, time pretty much becomes our own."

"How long d'you think it's going to take to get to Scotland?" asked Nat.

I shook my head dubiously. "I honestly don't know. I've driven there nonstop in ten, maybe twelve, hours, but that was under normal circumstances, averaging seventy miles an hour. With things the way they are now, who knows? Maybe a week, possibly longer. It's all down to detours and obstacles."

"We're well equipped," said Roger. "As long as we keep safe, then it's as Jules said: Time doesn't matter."

"Any idea where we might settle?" Linda asked.

"A few," I said. "Definitely in the west, maybe Torridon or Applecross or somewhere around Loch Maree. It depends on the conditions up there."

"I'm guessing you've been there before?" Charlie asked, sipping coffee after finishing his sandwich.

"You could say that," I said.

"We'll find out soon enough," Jules said, "and I, for one, am looking forward to it."

There was a chorus of agreement.

"Never too old for an adventure, eh, Old Man?" I winked at him.

"Absolutely. And..." Jules began.

"Not so much of the 'old'!" Charlie, Nat, and I finished.

"I think the rain's slowing," Linda said.

"You're right. It is," I agreed. "We've still got a few hours; let's pack up and get moving."

"Tina! Tina!" Sally's voice was frantic as she looked around the coach.

We all turned as one. Sally was looking around the underpass, worry creasing her face as she called Tina's name again.

"Sal?" I queried.

"It's Tina," Sally said worriedly. "She's not on the coach. I checked the toilet, searched the other seats, and she's not there."

Five

Six

"Did anyone see her get off the coach?" I asked.
  No one had.

"I asked the children who remained on the bus, and no one saw her leave, and Peter was asleep," Sally said.

"She must have gone back along the motorway. We would have seen her otherwise," I said. "Tom, take your boys and go back along the carriageway. Charlie, take Terry, Alan, and Jeff, go the opposite way in case Tina managed to slip by us unnoticed. Roger, go ahead of Tom, and Linda can go with Charlie."

Everyone hurried off, and Tina's name immediately echoed in the rain.

"Jules, you come with me and Nat; we'll go up onto the overpass."

Sally touched my arm, her voice trembling from worry. "Find her, Adam."

"We will. Don't worry. She can't be far. You, Julie, and the others watch over the children, okay?"

The rain was warm, almost pleasant on the skin. Within minutes, we were all soaked, but at least it was easing off. The clouds were slowly dispersing, rolling sluggishly off to the south and taking the rain with them. The thunder became a distant rumble.

The search parties fanned out, calling Tina's name as they went. The grassy incline beside the overpass wasn't steep, but the rain had made the grass treacherously slick underfoot, giving very little traction. Despite this, Jules went up the slope like a gazelle; Nat and I brought up the rear. At the top, a small "A" road dissected the M25, flowing east to west. What road it was, I couldn't begin to guess. There was no sign of Tina.

"Look! Here!" Nat called out, kneeling by a prickly bush. A scrap of cloth hung limply from his spiny branches.

"It looks like a piece of Tina's robe," Jules replied.

"She went that way," I said, pointing north-west.

The land was pretty flat with no pathways or tracks, just open overgrown fields gone to seed from years of neglect. Across the field, there was a clump of bushes backed by a stand of oak trees. Vision was still limited as we struck out across the field. I was following a vague path through the long grass which looked as if something big had recently passed.

A hundred yards in, we found some footprints, fresh and filling up with falling rain. Jules stooped down and picked something up.

"It's her slipper. She definitely came this way," he said excitedly.

We called her name, anxiously hoping for a reply or some farther sign—nothing. Fields stretched all around us, hemmed in by wildly overgrown hedgerows. Thankfully, there was no sign of the vines. The ground was muddy, thirstily drinking the rainfall like a dehydrated sponge after the long drought. Blue skies were returning as the dark clouds moved on like sinister galleons sailing across the sky. The sun burst out, hitting the damp ground like a red-hot fire iron, and within minutes, steam rose like a fog as the heat baked the earth.

At the lip of a small dell, Jules stopped again, peering intently down the gentle dip. He was about thirty yards ahead of us, and we couldn't see what he was looking at.

"Tina!" Jules yelled suddenly. "Tina! Stop!"

He dropped out of sight as he ran down into the dell. Suddenly galvanised, Nat tore after him. I nearly went flying as I hit the damp grass of the dell at a sprint. Barely managing to keep my feet on the slope, I saw Tina heading for a clump of bushes, Jules and Nat in close pursuit.

All but flying down the slope, heedless of falling, I rushed after them, quickly closing the gap. For all his vigour, Jules was slowing as Nat started to gain on him.

"Tina! Stop!" Nat yelled frantically, urgency raising her voice several octaves. "Tina! The vines!"

Jules was still ahead of Nat, saving his breath for running; the old man's fitness was amazing. Tina was soaked to the skin; her robe, filthy with mud, clung wetly to her in heavy folds as she staggered toward the bushes, and the bushes were moving!

"Tina!" I shouted, putting on a spurt.

With horror, I realised the vines were all around us, young, newly formed, and still growing but just as deadly. The sibilant rustling filled the air. Stray tendrils whipped out as us as we passed, but thankfully, they fell far too short.

Tina stumbled to a halt, swaying drunkenly on unsteady legs, her fingers entwined in her lank, wet hair which hung over her slim shoulders in thick strands. The bush in front of her burst into frenzied motion; the vines writhed and lashed out just as Jules reached her.

"Look out!" Nat screamed as a long tendril flicked out.

With speed that belied his age, Jules grabbed Tina, twisting round and pulling her back. The vine slashed down but missed her. Two more vines lashed out as Jules hauled the unresisting Tina out of harm's way, and they tumbled onto the wet grass.

Nat skidded to a stop on her knees and turned Tina over. I got there two seconds later.

"Is she alright?" gasped Jules, his chest heaving.

Nat breathed a sigh of relief. "Yeah, she's okay, but she's burning up."

I touched my hand to Tina's face and flinched at the fierce heat emanating from her skin.

"We need to get her back fast," I said, getting to my feet.

I took the radio from my belt and thumbed open a channel.

"This is Adam. We've got Tina; she's fine. We're on our way back."

Nat helped me get Tina to her feet, and between us, we helped her walk. Wearily, Jules followed.

"I don't know what you're on, Old Man," I said over my shoulder, "but whatever it is, I'll have two."

Jules looked at me wanly, his dark complexion a little grey. "Good living and a happy heart," he said a little breathlessly. "And less of the 'old,' if you don't mind!"

We were met at the top of the embankment by Tom Taylor and his sons. They took Tina from us and gently got her down the slope; her head lolled limply, since she had passed out. We followed them down, and Linda met me at the bottom.

"Is she okay?" she asked worriedly.

"She's got a fever. She was burning up, which probably explains her delirium. It was close; if Jules hadn't pulled her back, the vines would have gotten her."

I looked back at Jules as he stood at the bottom of the slope by the concrete pillar near the edge of the overpass.

"I'll make sure Tina knows who saved her..."

A tingle rippled over my skin as I saw Jules sway slightly, his body rigid, as stiff as a mannequin, his face was ashen grey, and his eyes sunk deep in their sockets.

"Jules?"

He tried to smile, and a low sound escaped his lips—a failed attempt to laugh. Sweat coursed down his face as he looked down at his outspread hands before looking back at me. His knees came unhinged, his legs turned to rubber, and he pitched forward. I barely had time to catch him before he hit the concrete.

"Jules!" Fear leapt into my throat as I laid him gently to the ground, my fingers reaching for the pulse in his throat.

"What the fuck...?" I stared at the copious blood covering my entire hand.

I hefted Jules up; the back of his shirt was soaked in blood.

"No, no, no, no," I moaned as I tore the shirt open.

There were at least eight puncture wounds, swollen, inflamed, leaking blood.

"Jules…"

He gripped my hand, and this time, he managed a smile.

"It's okay," he whispered, his voice rasping over dry lips.

"No…" I said lowly, my throat tightening.

"Better me than Tina," he said. "Now, I can finally rest." He closed his eyes and slowly opened them. "Celeste is waiting for me. I can see her waving at me." His smile was so beautiful, and his eyes shone. His bony fingers tightened in my hand. "It's up to you now, Adam," he said fiercely. "You look after our people; you take them home. Promise me! Take them home…"

"I'll keep them safe, Old Man, I promise."

I took his hand in both of mine. His eyes closed again slowly, and he sighed contently.

"I told you…" he said, "not so much of the 'old'…"

I wanted to scream, to rant, to rave at the unfairness of it all. I don't know how long I knelt there holding Jules' lifeless hand, unaware that the others had gathered around us. I was vaguely aware of people crying and holding one another. Then I felt a hand on my shoulder—Linda.

It was too much. This wasn't right. Jules was supposed to be there in Scotland. He said so himself. He was looking forward to it, to living the free life. He was my sounding board, my advisor ... my friend. He was the patriarch, and I didn't know what I was going to do without his dry wit and steadying influence.

Linda took my arm, and Sally held the other, her face wet with tears.

"Come on, Adam, come away. Charlie will look after Jules."

Rising to my feet, I shrugged them off.

"No," I said, "I will."

I sat with my back to the rear wheel of the taxi. I was numb. I'd carefully wrapped Jules' body in a tarpaulin and laid him in the back of the cab; though, in all honesty, I didn't remember doing it. I wasn't going to leave him here. I would take him somewhere nice, with a view, on a hill. He would have a proper funeral. During one of our many talks on the roof of the Block, one where we weren't actually arguing, he had told me that he didn't want to be buried when he passed, especially now; he thought the earth was contaminated. "No, I'll go to the flames," he had told me. *That's what I'll do*, I silently promised him, somehow, somewhere. For Jules.

My heart was sick.

"Adam, we have to move." Linda's voice seemed tiny, distant even though she was kneeling right next to me. "Are you listening to me?" she asked.

I wasn't.

"You can't do this. You're not being fair. Jules was our friend too, Charlie's, Sally's, mine ... all of us."

The drone of her voice paused.

"You promised him; Nat told me. You promised you would see us all safe."

My inner voice told me it was true, but the outer self didn't care; it just wanted to be left alone.

"Adam?"

"He saved my life," a voice said. I didn't realise it was my own. "I was ill, lost. Jules found me, made me well. I nearly ran him down..."

It seemed so long ago.

"I didn't even know the thorns had poisoned him until he fell into my arms. He saved Tina, which was more than I did. I may have let her down, but Jules didn't. He never let anyone down."

"Then keep your promise and lead us out of here; it's what Jules wanted. These people, our people, are depending on us, on you," Linda persisted. "We've come too far, sacrificed too much to stop now..."

"Linda," Charlie interrupted, "I can hear engines; they're coming this way."

Seven

The underpass was filled with lights and dancing shadows. The sound of engines reverberated through the confined space, bouncing off the naked stone walls. Doors opened, men were shouting, their boots crunching on the concrete. I didn't see it, but I sensed Linda and Charlie move away from me. My head was down and my eyes closed.

There was talking, brief exchanges, and then I was surrounded by people again.

"He's in no state to drive," Charlie said.

"I'll take the cab," Tom replied.

"He can ride with me in the van. I don't think the kids should see him like this," said Alan.

"Where are they taking us?" Julie asked.

"The sergeant said some sort of temporary way station at South Mimms. They weren't very forthcoming with their information," Charlie answered.

Someone barked orders, an unfamiliar voice.

I heard all of this through a dense fog. I heard but didn't care, couldn't connect. I didn't want to connect. *I made a mistake, a terrible mistake. I should have left when I had the chance, gone my own way, and never burdened myself with the responsibility of so many souls, so many friends: Jules, Tina. What was I thinking?*

"They want us to move out," Alan said. "Help me get him up."

I felt hands on me, lifting me to my feet. I let them lead me. I didn't know where, and I didn't much care.

The seat belt was clicked into place as I sat in the passenger seat of the smaller van. Night had fallen, and the road was pitch black; only the lancing beams of headlights gave illumination as I lay my throbbing head against the cool glass of the side window and stared blankly through the dirty pane. I don't recall how long we drove; I think I dozed for a while.

Only the bright glare of the massive arc lights penetrating my fog-shrouded brain told me we had arrived. Several nondescript huts lined the road. Situated on either side of the gates, crude wooden towers topped with sentry boxes watched over the huts; searchlights blazed over the area. Beyond, a huge camp was revealed; a sea of tents of various sizes and colours stretched out into the darkness.

We drove into a large parking area filled with military vehicles, mainly troop carriers and armoured cars. Alan pulled up beside the coach as it disgorged our people, gazing about in awe. It had been almost a year since they had seen so many people together in one place.

Soldiers directed them toward a large tent; Charlie and Julie led the way. I had no resistance in me as I was helped from the van and led into the tent. It was warm inside, almost stuffy; the scent of many bodies, sweat, and damp clothes filled my nostrils. I found myself sitting on a military camp bed in a quiet corner. Familiar voices were all around me, then a new voice asking who was in charge. Charlie and Linda spoke up. I laid down and put my arm over my eyes.

"We've got to do something." The urgency in Charlie's voice woke me.

I hadn't realised I had drifted off.

"They're going to hold us here and evacuate us with the rest of the people," continued Charlie.

"We need to tell them about Inferno," Nat urged.

"No," Linda disagreed. "If we tell them, they'll definitely hold us while they check it out. If anything, it might make those in charge of the firebombing execute the plan sooner."

"But we have to say something. All these people..." Nat said.

"We can't say anything yet, not until our people are safely away; they come first," said Linda. "I know that sounds harsh, but it's our only chance."

"Can't we just try and break out?" Charlie asked. "There's no real security, no fences or gates. We just get in the coach and go."

"The road's blocked with army trucks," Jeff said. "While you were talking with the Major, I had a little look around. I didn't see any other security; the soldiers just seem to be keeping order, and everybody is very placid and compliant."

"How do we convince Major Saunders to let us go on our way?" Julie asked.

"I don't know," Linda said. "They haven't attempted any sort of search on our vehicles, and their medics checked out Peter and Tina. I think Saunders just wants to make the evacuation as orderly as possible."

"D'you think he knows about Inferno?" asked Charlie.

"If he does, then he's been misinformed," Linda replied. "I don't think he knows the danger is imminent."

"They saw Jules' body in the back of the cab," Tom said. "They want to take him and put him with their casualties. I think the camp chaplain is planning a mass funeral before the evacuation begins."

I was on my feet in an instant.

"No," I said emphatically.

Startled, they all looked at me.

"They're not taking Jules, and we're not staying here," I said.

"Adam, they won't let us through," Linda said. "Major Saunders, the officer in charge, is waiting for his superiors to return from London. As acting commander, he is not authorised to begin the evacuation; he is to hold the refugees here."

"We're not refugees; we're a cohesive community who are relocating north, as per the evacuation protocols given to us," I said. "Where's Saunders?"

Exchanging nervous glances with the others, Charlie went to the tent flap. It was obvious they thought I was still in shock. And maybe I was, but I could hear Jules' voice in my head: "You look after our people; you take them home. Promise me! Take them home." I would not break my promise.

"Hey mate," Charlie said to the soldier standing just outside the tent. "We need to talk to the major again."

The soldier looked sourly at Charlie, thought about it, and said, "I don't know if he's free. Give me a minute." He disappeared.

"Adam, are you okay?" Linda asked me quietly.

I looked into the conflicting emotions roiling inside my head, still not making any real sense of them.

"I don't know..." I said, rubbing my face. "Yes. Just..." I searched for the word. "Tired."

"I know we're asking a lot of you, Adam, and I know it puts a terrible strain on you, but you're our best chance of survival, of getting through this nightmare. We are here for you, to support you, all of us," Linda said.

"She's right, mate. We're behind you one hundred percent," added Charlie.

"Despite my mistakes?" I asked.

"Mistakes?" said Julie, puzzled.

"Kaminsky, Tina, and now Jules..."

"What the hell are you talking about?" Linda said indignantly. "None of that's your fault. It just happened."

"It happened because of me," I answered bleakly. "I should have seen it coming."

"Crap!" Charlie said fiercely. "Jules and Tina would be the first to tell you that, and you know it! Linda's right, you're best qualified to get us through, but you're not alone. We're family, remember? We all take the responsibility."

Before I could say anything further, the tent flapped open and a tall thin officer stepped in, closely followed by a sergeant. He looked at us with a suspicious frown. The name tag pinned to the right breast of his dark green jacket identified him as Saunders.

"What's this all about?" he demanded. "I thought I had already made myself clear."

"Not to me, you haven't," I said, stepping forward.

Saunders regarded me with dark brown intelligent eyes, looking both suspicious and surprised at the same time.

"And you are?" he asked without missing a beat.

"This group's spokesman," I answered.

"You weren't at the meeting earlier," Saunders said.

"I was ... indisposed," I said. "My friends told me of your decision to hold us here, and I want to know by whose authority?"

"This area is under martial law," Saunders said. "As acting commander of this facility, the safety and wellbeing of it and the refugees falls under my remit."

"We are neither part of this installation nor refugees. We were evacuated from our homes, but we have lived as a community for the last eleven months. We prospered, and we were secure. It was only when we encountered one of your lot that we decided evacuating further was probably the best course of action. We left London and were told to make for the North Corridor, where we would be allowed to pass without hindrance."

"Who told you this?" Saunders asked.

"Captain James Williams, Special Recon and Expedition Force," I said, quietly pleased at the reaction on the major's face. "I see you know him."

"I do, and I know of his record," admitted Saunders.

"Then you'll know of Operation Inferno?" I asked.

Saunders became guarded. "Williams told you about Inferno?"

"I was at his camp when he got the orders to start the evacuation. That's when he told us to head north. Major, we're leaving right now, and I would appreciate it if you removed the barricades from the road."

"You're right," he said. "I have no real authority to hold you, but I would strongly advise against striking north on your own. You have two injured, one dead, and the children to consider."

"All that has been taken into consideration. We know the risks, and we reached a joint decision to go on. We work as a democracy."

"A family," Charlie added.

Despite the conflicting emotions flowing through my brain, I supressed a smile. God Bless Charlie...

"We thank you for all that you've done for us, our injured, and for the food. We will take care of our ... casualty." The word was hard for me to say.

Saunders regarded us stonily for a few seconds. "Very well," he said, taking a deep breath. "Sergeant, have the barricades removed. Open the road."

The sergeant saluted and left the tent.

"Major, one last thing," I said. "Take my advice: don't linger. Forget waiting for your superiors; I don't think they're coming. Get this evacuation moving today, right now. The deadline Captain Williams quoted for the commencement of Operation Inferno might not be one hundred percent reliable. There are a lot of people here; you need to move them out."

At that moment, I realised Saunders was already having the same thoughts. He hid it well, army stiff upper lip, but I saw the doubt in his eyes.

"Why north?" he asked suddenly.

I thought about it for a second and decided there was no reason not to tell him my theory.

"I believe the vines and the Creeps have an aversion to the cold, which is why our climate is changing, getting hotter day by day. Scotland's cold."

"Very astute," Saunders said pensively.

He stepped to the tent flap as if he was going to leave, paused, and then turned back to me.

"I'd like you to meet someone before you leave. It may be to your advantage," he said.

"Time's tight."

"I understand. It won't take long, and I really think you ought to hear what this man has to say."

"Linda? Charlie?"

"A few more minutes won't make much difference," Linda said, "especially if it helps us."

"It might," reiterated Saunders. "Then you'll be free to go. I give you my word."

"Nat, get everybody ready to leave," I said. Then turning back to Saunders, "Lead on."

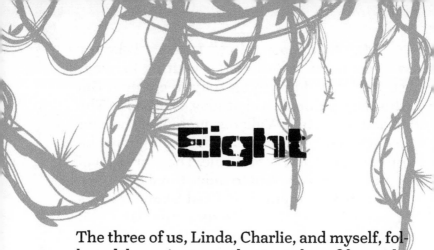

Eight

The three of us, Linda, Charlie, and myself, followed the major to another tent about fifty yards away. We entered and found we were in some sort of mobile laboratory. Benches crowded with plants, alembics, microscopes, and a ton of other scientific paraphernalia filled the limited space. The smell of fresh earth was strong.

"Professor?" Saunders called.

A big man, maybe early fifties, stepped out from behind a bench filled with broad leaf plants. Heavily bearded with black curly hair swept back from a broad forehead, he regarded us with keen brown eyes over the top of a pair of rimless glasses perched on the tip of a thin nose.

"What is it?" His voice was rich, quiet, but it carried easily.

"Professor Jennings, I would like you to meet Adam Blake and his two friends, Linda Stephens and Charles Donovan."

"Charlie," said Charlie.

Saunders ignored him and turned to me. "This is Professor Paul Jennings. I think you'll find he shares some of your theories concerning the vines."

"Theories? What theories?" asked Jennings.

I told him.

"That's interesting, very interesting," he said after I had finished; it was like he was actually talking to himself. "And you think going to Scotland with its inherent weather conditions will hold the vines and these creatures at bay?"

"That's the plan," I said.

"You're right, of course, up to a point," Jennings said, "but have you considered climate change?"

"I have," I answered, "but there's nothing I can do about that."

"No, no, of course not, and that's where the problem lies. Somehow, someway, the vines and/or the creatures are causing the climate change, and when they succeed, I don't think we'll be able to prevent them from overrunning the entire world."

"Well, that's comforting," Charlie said sourly.

"Do you know where they come from? How they got here?" asked Linda.

"Only conjecture," Jennings replied, "but they are definitely extra-terrestrial."

"Alien?" I asked.

"Yes," Jennings said without hesitation as if was the most normal thing in the world. "I was part of a think-tank in Whitehaven, that's in Cumbria. We explored all sorts of theories concerning the origins of the black Dust. The most favoured, though by no means definitive, is that the Dust simply floated through space, propelled by solar winds or possibly the magnetic pull of gravity. Its actual origin is impossible to determine."

"And the vines?" I asked.

"Yes, that's where it gets very interesting." His enthusiasm was a little unsettling. "We gathered samples of the black Dust, lots of samples. On examination, my colleagues and I discovered that within the mass of Dust, there were several types of spores, seeds if you will. I have never seen anything like them. We believe the creatures and the vines are the products of these spores."

"Are you saying the Creeps, the creatures, are plant-based?" I asked incredulously.

"Yes and no," Jennings answered. "Come, let me show you."

We moved deeper into the tent where a bench full of mason jars lined a back wall.

"Holy shit!" Charlie gasped.

Several of the jars contained the bodies of small Creeps, a fraction of the size of the one's we had encountered on the Queen Elizabeth Second Bridge. I remembered what Terry Moore had said about the creatures that attacked his family in Dartford: "...no bigger than cats."

"They start out as seeds," Jennings began, "then they grow into buds. But then, on some genetic level we don't yet understand, they metamorphose into flesh and blood. We have established that the creatures and the vines are symbiotically linked; where there's one, you will find the other nearby, protecting each other, feeding each other, thereby ensuring the survival of their species."

"What triggers their growth?" Linda asked, peering into one of the jars. The liquid was murky; its contents a vague shape.

"Contact with the soil, especially wet soil," said Jennings.

"Was the storm following the deluge caused by the black Dust?" I asked.

"Quite possibly," agreed the professor. "It certainly helped initiate their propagation."

Charlie looked at me, his expression downcast. "So, it's possible that Scotland is infected already?" he asked.

"Not necessarily," Jennings interceded. "There's no doubt the black Dust fell on Scotland. It was probably a worldwide phenomenon, but the cold conditions would have prevented the spores from germinating. Of course, the hotter it gets, the likelihood of them being activated increases. Although, preliminary tests indicate that if they do not germinate within a certain period, they die."

"How long a period?" I asked.

"Approximately two weeks," said Jennings, "but please remember, this is mainly hypothesis. And there's something else you should know..."

"I'm not sure we want to know," Linda said bleakly.

Jennings carried on regardless. "A single teacup of black Dust contains thousands of spores of five distinct types. Two of the spores we have identified as the creatures and the vines, but the other ... we have no idea."

"Other life forms?" Linda asked.

"A distinct possibility," Jennings said in his irritating, matter-of-fact voice.

"What can we do to protect ourselves?" I asked, somehow knowing what Jennings was going to say.

"Frankly, nothing," said the professor, realising my fears. "Keep away from the vines. The spores are practically indestructible in their dormant state. Once they germinate, they can be destroyed by fire or industrial-strength weed killer but only in the early stages. Once they start to mature, killing them becomes exponentially harder. The same with the creatures, which grow at an accelerated rate."

"We've had experience with that," I said.

"I would be reluctant to cultivate any land that contains dormant spores. If the land has been frozen, then it will probably be safe."

"So, what do we do?" Charlie asked, defeat edged his voice.

"Stick to the plan," I answered immediately. "It's all we've got. I still think Scotland's our best bet."

I turned to Professor Jennings. "Thanks, you've been a great help," I said.

"Not at all," he said, shaking my hand. "I only wish it had been better news for you."

Eight

Nine

Major Saunders walked with us for a while after we left Jennings' tent. No one was saying anything as we walked to the command tent; it was a lot to take in.

"I wish you luck," he said; his smile was strained.

I shook his hand. "Same to you, Major. Thanks."

He shrugged, and with a short nod to Linda and Charlie, disappeared into the tent.

"Well, that was a kick in the nuts," Charlie said as we walked back to our vehicles.

"It wasn't anything we didn't already suspect," I said. "Saunders has enough problems without adding us to the mix; he's more than glad to get us out of his hair. Let's get moving before something else happens to change his mind."

I thought dawn was still three or four hours away, but I wasn't sure; I'd lost all track of time when I was wallowing in self-pity. I silently cursed my weakness. *Jules deserved better.* I pushed the unwanted thoughts away, trying to concentrate on the situation at hand. I didn't much like the idea of driving at night, but right now, our choices were limited.

"Get everyone into the coach, same formation as before. Let's not hang around," I said.

"Are you okay?" Charlie asked, concern tinged his voice. "You seem edgy."

"I will be when everyone stops asking me the same damned question," I snapped. Then I stopped, sighing heavily. "Charlie, I'm sorry."

"It's okay, mate. I get it. Maybe we can talk later."

"No, Charlie, I really am sorry. Jules meant a lot to all of us. He was a friend to all of us. I shouldn't be taking my grief out on you and everyone else. It's just that I didn't intend to get close; I didn't want to get close..."

"That's what being friends is all about, Adam. That's what's gonna make sure we all survive this craziness. Family."

Engines started and motorbikes roared into life as I got into the cab. I felt my heart clench when I glimpsed the dark bundle on the rear seat. I quickly looked away. Maybe Charlie was right, maybe we needed that connection, that bond, to help us pull through, but it was contrary to my nature; I was a loner. Then I realised *was,* was the operative word. It was hard to deal with.

"The road should be clear," I spoke into the mike. "Roger, Linda, lead off. Don't stop for anything."

Linda looked over at me as she sat astride her bike. She nodded, flipped down her visor, and gunned her engine. I fell in behind her and Roger, and Alan pulled out behind me.

"Keep close till we get clear," I said.

Despite the early hour, a crowd had gathered on the roadside to watch us pass. There were a lot of curious people wondering what was going on and who we were. Some of them were having animated conversations; there was a lot of pointing and angry gesturing. There were also a lot of weary expressions. Hopelessness and despair were etched into the lined and dirty faces of men, women, and even some children. Seeing the haunted eyes of lost people, my heart went out to them. I felt sick, but I couldn't help them, regardless of how I felt. And I knew the others were feeling the same. As harsh as it was, these lost souls were Saunders' responsibility. They had to look to him to bring them to safety, and I sincerely hoped he would act and soon.

"Jesus, there's thousands of them," Charlie said over the radio.

The army tents fell behind as the main enclave gave way to the civilian camp, a canvas city with tents and shelters of all shapes and sizes. The tents were in ordered rows, line after line of them, hundreds of colours, bleached almost white in the glare of the arc lamps. How Major Saunders had accomplished this miracle was a marvel of organization. It reminded me of pictures I had seen of Roman military camps: contained, ordered, precise.

The blockade trucks had been removed and were now parked along the hard shoulder. Soldiers watched as we drove through; some even waved. Guilt nagged at me. I wanted to tell them to leave, now, and get as far away from here as possible, but it was pointless, I had done all I could, but I still felt selfish like I was betraying them. Once more, I prayed Major Saunders would take my warning on board.

"Look at the skyline," Linda's voice broke into my thoughts.

To the north, a red-orange glow permeated the night sky, low, stretching from horizon to horizon in an unearthly bloom.

"Don't tell me that's Inferno?" came Charlie's voice.

"No," I answered. "I don't know what that is, but it's not Inferno. There'd be no doubt if it was. Besides, that's north, and London is behind us."

The two-lane road became three as we got onto the M1 motorway, passing out through Hendon. Surprisingly, the road was clear; I had expected a lot more obstructions. There were still a lot a vehicles, but they were situated on the left of the motorway. It didn't take a genius to figure out that this was more of Major Saunders work—The North Corridor. I silently thanked the man.

"Adam, is Nat with you?" Charlie asked.

"No, isn't she on the coach?" I answered.

"No," Charlie said. "Jeff, Alan?"

"Not with me," said Jeff.

"Nor me," echoed Alan.

"Shit," I cursed. "She's stayed back at the camp, probably trying to convince Saunders to pack up and leave."

"Surely not?" Julie asked.

"She spoke to me about warning Saunders about Inferno before we left. I told her he already knew and that I had strongly hinted to Saunders that the timetable wasn't safe.

Obviously, Nat thought that wasn't enough. Let's pull over," I said.

We gathered by the coach.

"Why would Nat go back if Saunders was aware of Inferno?" asked Linda.

"I don't know. Maybe she had the same thought as me. I'm not sure Saunders believed me when I told him about Williams being unstable. They knew each other, and I think he trusts Williams' judgement."

"Meaning he might not evacuate straight away?" asked Linda.

"Exactly," I said.

"What do we do?" Charlie asked.

"I'll have to go back for her," I said, "but I don't want to take the cab."

"I can go," Linda said. "It'll be faster."

"No, I'll take the van; Alan can take the cab."

Linda didn't look happy.

"Can we have a word?" Linda said.

I knew what was coming.

"Are you sure about this?" she asked after we had walked a short distance out of earshot. "You've had a shock and been under a lot of pressure..."

"And I'm good with it," I interrupted her. "You're right. Jules' death hit me hard. He kept me grounded, kept me on track, and losing him was gutting, but I'm dealing with it. I wasn't happy about being responsible for all our people, but Jules made me see that's the way it is, whether I like it or not. He made me see beyond myself and my needs.

"So, I'll go and get Nat," I continued. "You help Charlie and Julie and just keep heading north. I'll catch up."

"Adam…"

I took her in my arms, holding her close and feeling the softness of her hair on my cheek.

"I'm okay, Lin. I promise." I kissed the top of her head. "I'll be back before you know it."

She looked up at me and quickly kissed my mouth. "You'd better be," she said.

The drive back to the camp was fast, probably because I had my foot to the floor the whole way. On arrival, the place was alive with flashlight beams scything around the canvas city, augmenting the arc lights watching over the camp. Whether the order had been given or not, it seemed people were preparing to leave en masse. Army vehicles lined the roadway, and soldiers helped civilians to board, clutching their meagre belongings in suitcases, backpacks, even plastic bags.

Easing my way through the tumult, I reached the main command tent. The entrance was unguarded, so I breezed straight in. Major Saunders sat, straight backed behind the table doubling as a desk.

"I wondered how long it would be before you turned up," he said without preamble.

"Where is she?" I asked equally as blunt.

Saunders nodded to a soldier who had appeared behind me. With a brief salute, the soldier disappeared into the night.

"Is it true?" Saunders asked.

In that moment, I knew he had not been given the full intel on Inferno, and the realisation had shaken him. His trust and dependence on higher command, developed over long years of disciplined duty and service, had crumbled within minutes.

"I don't know," I said honestly. "I think so. Williams seemed a little … detached when he told me about the evacuation. He didn't seem to grasp the logistics of the task."

"The time element," Saunders stated.

"Exactly."

"And you think Inferno will go ahead regardless of the refugee situation?"

"I'm not prepared to take that chance," I said, "and neither should you. I prefer to think there's been a massive communications breakdown because the alternative doesn't bear thinking about."

"You think Central Command now regard London and the refugees as collateral damage?" he asked.

"Do you?" I bounced the question back at him. "I don't think it matters. You are here, you know the situation, and neither of us should take the risk."

Saunders pondered this as the soldier returned with Nat.

"We need to go," I said as she entered the tent.

"Not until I say so," Saunders said, standing up.

I squared off to him, looking straight into his face.

"You think you can stop us?" I asked.

"One word from me and I'll have a security detail in here before you can blink," Saunders said.

"And you'll be in here with a desperate man with a gun," I answered, wishing I was as cool as I was trying to sound. "Let's not make this

personal, Major. Our goals are the same. What Nat told you changes nothing. I appreciate your help, especially with the professor, and I wish I had been a little more forthcoming with my suspicions regarding Inferno, but I had my people to consider."

He contemplated by statement, visibly relaxing as he decided I was right.

"You're determined to go to Scotland?" he asked.

"Just as fast as we can," I said.

"I am going to direct the evacuation toward Norfolk; there are several military bases there: Robertson Barracks, Barham, Bodney. We'll find refuge there." Saunders stepped around the desk. "You can come with us if you prefer."

"No, like I said, our plans are laid. I wish you luck, Major."

"Likewise, and young lady..."

"Nat," she replied.

"Nat, thank you for your selflessness. I ... *we* really do appreciate it."

"No problem, Major," Nat said. "You can prove it by getting these people to safety."

"That was irresponsible," I said to Nat as soon as we were back on the road.

"I just couldn't walk away, Adam. I had to try. And I was right; Saunders only half-believed you about Williams. He was trying to get confirmation as we left," Nat said. "I won't apologise for trying to help these people."

"Like the bikers back at the Block?" I said.

"Everyone deserves a chance, good or bad. Those people back there are innocent. You said it yourself: survival is everything."

"You're preaching to the converted, Nat," I said with a smile. "But I swear, your altruism is going to get us into serious trouble one day."

"Us?" she said, eyebrows raised.

"Did you think I was just going to leave you behind?" I asked.

"Well, I was kind of hoping you wouldn't." She grinned.

Ten

The farther we got from London, the better I felt. I had no idea how far the range was of a thermo baric bomb or how many they would drop. Speed and distance seemed to be our best defence.

"What's all that?" Nat said, pointing at the red glow to the north.

"I don't know," I said. "It started about an hour ago; it looks like fire."

"Fire? But it stretches for miles," said Nat.

"Yeah," I agreed. "After months of baking hot sun and little to no rain, the entire countryside is like a tinderbox. I doubt the storm earlier made any real difference. If that is a fire, then there will be no stopping it; it will burn whatever gets in its way."

"Oh my God," breathed Nat.

Dawn was breaking just as we spotted the convoy up ahead. They had made good time. Hemel Hempstead lay just ahead, putting us about thirty miles outside of London. I was pretty sure we were safe. As we gained on them, the coach started to pull over. The motorway was relatively clear as all our vehicles came together.

"I was getting worried," Charlie stated.

"I think Saunders believed us in the end," I said. "Nat's efforts probably helped sway him, though I reckon he thought he should start moving regardless of our warnings. I just hope they get out in time."

"I'm sure they will," Julie said, none too confidently. "But you, young lady, need to stop trying to right every wrong."

Nat just shrugged and smiled wanly.

"We've already had that conversation," I cut in, "though I'm not sure it sank in."

"Probably not," Julie said, hugging the abashed Nat. "But next time, give us a little warning, eh?"

"Is everyone okay?" I asked.

"Yeah, tired mostly. It's been a hectic night. The children are restless and hungry," said Sally. "What about you?"

"I'm good, Sal," I said, trying to smile but not quite making it. "I'm sorry that I lost it for a while there."

"You're allowed," Sally said brightly, touching my arm affectionately. "But we've got a crowd of hungry children who just want to be fed."

"Let's get to the next junction; it's only a couple of miles. We'll stop and rest for a couple of hours and have breakfast," I said.

It was junction eight, Hemel Hempstead. We parked under an overpass and set up some cooking fires in portable barbeques. The children were eager to burn off their excess energy after being cooped up for so long. Trish and Joan kept a close watch on them while Sally and Julie, helped by some of the others, prepared breakfast.

I sat with Linda at the edge of the motorway overlooking the surrounding fields which were running rampant with hedgerows and waist-high grasses. Vines weren't apparent, but I was fairly certain they were lurking in the nearby copses and woodlands surrounding us.

I felt a lot better. Linda was resting her head on my shoulder and holding onto my arm as we sat in comfortable silence. The day grew brighter and the temperature began to soar though the heat wasn't stopping the kids from running about and squealing with delight in the shade of the underpass.

"I guess time's our own now," Linda mused.

"Yeah, I guess so. Now, we're clear of the city. There's no immediate rush, but I won't be entirely at peace till we reach Scotland."

"You're worried it's going to be like the rest of the country?" Linda asked.

"It's a distinct possibility, but we'll see," I said. "Right now ... I'm hungry."

"Wait, just a minute," Linda said.

She moved into my arms and kissed me, not just a peck but a real, meaningful kiss. I held her tightly as she clung to me, returning her kisses.

"We need to do this more often," she whispered in my ear.

"I'm not sure I can promise you a nice house and a life of ease and happiness," I said.

"A bothy and a double bed will suit me just fine," she said and kissed me again.

Peter Hogan, helped by Teresa and Terry, stepped down gingerly from the coach. He grimaced at every step, his swollen face still black and blue with livid bruising. He held his ribs as he made it to the ground with a deep sigh of relief.

"About time you stopped lazing around," Charlie called playfully.

Julie elbowed him in the ribs.

"Come and sit with us, Peter," Julie said. "Ignore the clown; he isn't funny!"

Charlie made a face.

We were all seated around a barbeque, though we hardly needed the extra heat. The air was redolent with the smell of bacon, sausages, and coffee. Julie helped Peter to a box, having declined one of the camp chairs, claiming it didn't have enough support.

"You might laugh, Charlie," Peter said once he was settled into a comfortable position, "but the coach was closing in on me. You have no idea what a total relief it is to get out of that bloody bed."

"Just don't get any notions about getting up any time soon," chided Sally. "You got a bit more healing to do yet."

Peter scowled. "I'm fine, Sal. I don't need any more rest."

"Yeah and pigs fly," she retorted.

Everyone laughed.

"Talking of pigs, that smells good," Peter said, eying the bacon on the barbeque.

"Let me make you a sandwich," offered Julie. "I'm afraid there's no butter, and there's not

much more bacon left, so you'd better make the most of it."

It was good just to sit and shoot the breeze. We were all healing, spiritually and physically, and being together like this was a real tonic. I noticed several eyes drifting southward, a cloud of worry reflected in concerned expressions as thoughts of the doomed London crossed their minds. None of us knew what to expect or what Operation Inferno actually meant, and everyone was obviously fearing the worst.

"I think we are well clear of the danger area," I said, attempting to allay their fears. "Moving on is probably a good idea though; let's put as much distance between us and London as we can."

The eager acceptance of the suggestion spoke volumes.

"Adam, Roger and I want to ride ahead. That red glow is worrying me, and it might be a good idea to check it out before the rest of the convoy get there."

"I don't know, Lin..." I began.

"It's better to look before we leap," said Roger. "Otherwise, what's the point in having scouts?"

There was no argument to that.

"Okay, but I want to come too," I said.

"You want the bike?" asked Roger, taken aback.

I laughed. "No, mate, I don't know how to ride one. I'll ride pillion with Linda."

"Get a spare helmet, and we'll be on our way," Linda said.

Leaving the others to clean up and follow on, the three of us headed north.

It had been a long time since I had been on the back of a motorbike. Thoughts of the long rides to the Lake District or down into Cornwall came to mind. Long, uncomfortable journeys on the pillion that left me aching and stiff. I didn't miss it. That being said, Linda was an excellent rider, and I did not have a moment's concern as she handled the bike well. The countryside flashed past as we thundered along the motorway. Ten miles on the scorched earth began, vast swathes of blackened countryside, burnt to ash, not a blade of grass remaining. Roger took exit ten, and we followed, stopping in the middle of the overpass straddling the motorway.

"That answers that question," said Roger, kicking the bike stand down and taking off his helmet.

I dismounted and gazed toward the glowing horizon.

"My God..." breathed Linda.

From horizon to horizon, fire blazed, consuming a landscape long deprived of rain and subjected to ever-increasing temperatures for the last ten months—a conflagration waiting to happen.

"It's totally out of control," Roger lamented.

"Who's left to control it?" I said darkly.

"Is it going to be a problem for us?" asked Linda.

"I don't think so," I said. "It's moving away from us on both fronts, going east and west. The M1 goes straight up through the middle."

"Maybe it's a good thing," Roger said. "At worst, it will destroy the vines and wipe out the Creep's habitat, maybe even the Creeps as well."

"We can only hope," I agreed.

"Do you think it was deliberate?" Linda asked.

"No way of knowing," I said. "I guess it really doesn't matter. It will burn itself out eventually, hopefully without any loss of life."

Walking across the bridge, I looked out over the landscape. Something caught my eye.

"What are you looking at?" asked Roger.

"That," I said, pointing.

About a mile off, like an emerald shining in a sea of black and grey ash, there was a low hill topped by a small copse of trees at its summit. It was hard to distinguish them at this distance, but they looked like birches. Miraculously, the fire hadn't touched the hill.

"That's amazing," said Roger.

"It's perfect," I said.

"For what?" Linda asked, puzzled.

"Jules," I said.

Eleven

FUNERAL

It's funny how fear can conjure up all sorts of demons, making events seem of apocalyptic proportions when nothing could be further from the truth. I knew we were in the middle of an apocalyptic event, and things didn't look good, so I wasn't decrying the serious ramifications of Operation Inferno, but when it came, in a weird way, it was a bit anticlimactic.

We were heading back to the group when there were several bright flashes to the south—flaming orange accompanied by dull thumps that were felt through the earth more than heard. The sky was filled with columns of dark grey and black smoke billowing on the horizon. I hadn't even seen or heard the aircraft, assuming the payload had been delivered by planes. Maybe the delivery method had been missiles. You say bombs; I think planes. From this distance, it didn't seem like much, but my heart was sick at the thought of all the people back there in the camp. I hoped they got out in time.

Linda stopped and pushed up her visor, eyes narrowed against the raging firestorm.

"I hope they got out," she murmured, echoing my thoughts.

"I'm sure they did," I said without conviction.

"Jesus, the whole bloody country's on fire," said Roger.

Everyone was looking south. The convoy was barely a mile from the underpass where we had breakfast. Lined up across the motorway, they watched in silence with the exception of an odd gasp as another bomb exploded in a rippling, orange-yellow blast. We left the encampment less than three hours ago. From their expressions, I could see Charlie, Julie, and the others were all thinking the same thing. They had their own misgivings, the overwhelming doubt that there was no way all those people cleared the area before the bombs dropped—some maybe but not all. The only hope I held, and it was slim, was that the bombs had targeted well beyond the camp's perimeter.

Wiping the sweat off my face with my forearm, I stood looking at the green hill. The day was particularly hot; the hard, light blue sky had turned into a merciless furnace. A small road ran around the base of the mound, and I'd been able to get close with the taxi and its precious burden. Getting Jules to the summit was going to be difficult, but I'd manage. Then it was just a matter of building the funeral pyre, and I was certain there would be plenty of deadfall among the trees.

I figured I would take a few hours absence from the convoy and catch up with them later once I was done. I figured wrong. I should have known better. Engines sounded behind me, a lot of engines. Turning, I saw the coach trundling along the narrow perimeter road toward the hill; it was led by the two motorcycles and followed by the vans. I waited as the convoy drew to a halt, and everyone tramped over the field toward me. A very disgruntled Sally was in front, and she definitely did not look happy.

"Just what do you think you are doing?" She laid into me before I had the chance to say anything, her eyes flashing. "Don't you think we all have the right to be here?"

"I..." The words stuck in my throat.

"It's not just about you," she continued. "Jules was a friend to all of us, more to some. If anything, I knew him the longest and was the closest. I think that allows me the right to see him on his last journey."

"I get that, Sal, but Jules didn't want to be buried; he said the ground was contaminated. I didn't think a crude funeral pyre would be to everyone's taste. Despite what you might have seen on TV or in the movies, it's quite stressful, especially for the kids."

"I agree, in part," she said. "It's not for children, but they still need to come to terms with their own loss. Jules was like a grandfather to them, the older kids especially. They deserve closure too."

"They could help gather wood for the pyre," said Tricia. "After the service, Joan and I will take them off before the actual cremation."

"We all want to say goodbye to Jules," Charlie said, "so we all should attend his funeral. If the actual cremation is too much for some, then they can help Tricia watch over the children."

I smiled. Truth be told, I was glad they all felt that way. A great weight was lifted from my heart.

"Okay, I was wrong, but I was only thinking of you," I said.

"Thinking's good," Julie said. "Talking's better."

Alan and Jeff built a stretcher with some tent poles and a tarpaulin while Julie and Sally dressed Jules with a blanket, leaving only his head visible. Even in death, he looked so serene and calm, as if he had discovered a marvellous secret on the other side. So many of us still felt the calming influence emanating from this remarkable man.

There were two fallen birch trees in the copse at the hills summit and a ton of deadfall. Using chain saws, Tom Taylor and his boys set about cutting the trunks into manageable lengths. Charlie and I built a pyre in a large clearing at the edge of the copse. We made it square with logs spanning the middle, and the children, helped by Terry, Teresa, Tricia, and Joan, tightly packed the remaining space with small branches and twigs. Finally, Charlie doused the whole affair with a liberal amount of petrol to ensure a fierce burn.

Reverently, we placed our friend on top of the pyre; it stood five feet tall and six feet square. Everyone stood silently in a circle, heads bowed, each lost in their own memories of Jules.

"He was our mentor," Linda began in a soft voice, "our leader, our counsellor. I didn't know him for long, but in that short time, we became close; that was Jules' power: a welcoming heart and an understanding ear. I am glad he was in my life. He touched us all with his humour, his wisdom, and his guidance. I will miss him."

The wind dropped, making everything still. The branches of the nearby birch trees stopped moving as if in deference; even the birds stopped singing.

"I was broken when Jules took me in," Teresa said, her dark eyes full of pain. "My world was devastated when my brother died during the black Dust. My mother died in my arms a short time after. I wanted to die too.

"But I didn't because Jules wouldn't let me. He showed me life, no matter how hard, is precious and should be treasured. He taught me to take one day at a time and learn from each day. He brought me out of the darkness. I will be eternally grateful to him and will never forget him."

"I was Jules' nurse for more years than I care to remember," Sally said. "He idolised and cherished his dear wife, Celeste. Like her name, she was his shining star," her voice cracked, and she coughed quietly. "It was a massive blow when Celeste passed; a lesser man might have crumbled, but Jules was a cantankerous,

old fool, and he wouldn't be beaten. Celeste wouldn't allow it."

A low rippling of tear-filled laughter resonated among us.

"Jules cared for people," Sally continued. "He always did. He saw only the good and excused the bad. We argued a lot, like cat and dog, but without rancour, without malice. I think the old sod mostly did it just to wind me up.

"I love you, Jules; you were the best of friends. Losing you has broken my heart, but I find comfort that you are finally where you belong, where your heart has always wanted to be, with your beloved Celeste."

Others spoke in quiet reverence, each with a different anecdote, some gem about Jules Robideaux that others may not have heard or known about. As the litany commenced, I stared at his face in repose, feeling the emptiness welling up inside again.

"When I met Jules," I began, "I nearly ran him down. In my defence, I was totally out of it. I thought I was dying. Jules and Sally brought me back from the dead. He was stubborn, and he sometimes saw the world through rose-tinted glasses. He always allowed you your point of view, whether he agreed or not. He had a way of guiding without patronising, and he showed me the way many times without ever saying, 'I told you so,' if I messed up.

"Even at the end, he gave his life without hesitation so that another might live. Because that was Jules. He was the best of us, certainly better than me. I will forever miss his steadying hand. Go on your final journey, Jules; know that you have touched all our lives and will forever live in our hearts. A dark world is now even darker without your shining light to illuminate our lives. I will keep the promise I made you ... on my life."

I was surprised to find my face wet with tears; there was a deep ache inside me.

After a few minutes of silence, Trish led the children quietly away to the farther side of the copse. Charlie produced a torch made from a birch branch and some sacking which was soaked in petrol and bound tightly with wire. He offered it to me, and I passed it on to Sally.

"You knew him the best," I said.

Sally nodded, her face creased with pain, tears coursing down her cheeks.

"Let's do it together," she said quietly.

Charlie sparked up his lighter, and the torch flared. Stepping forward, Sally and I plunged the branch deep into the pyre. It caught immediately, and we stepped back, watching with wet eyes as the flames engulfed our friend. The silence was as heavy as our hearts. The only sound was the crackling of the petrol-soaked wood as grey smoke reached up into the clear sky. Julie sobbed quietly in Charlie's arms. Terry and Teresa hugged one another. I felt Linda's arm encircle my waist as she laid her head on my shoulder.

It was too much for some of them; with bowed heads, they silently moved away through the trees until only Linda, Sally, Charlie, Julie, Terry, Teresa, and I remained. I think we were all numb with the suddenness of it all, the senselessness, just staring at the flames in mute grief.

"Let's go join the others," Linda said softly.

I realised we were alone.

"You go," I said. "I just need a little more time. It's okay, honest."

Linda's look of concern softened.

"I'll be there in a little while," I said.

I sat with my back to a birch tree, watching as the funeral pyre began to burn down. Dusk wasn't far off, but it was still very warm. The shock of it all had left me with no conscious thought in my head. The fire held my fascinated gaze. I smiled thinly as I recalled how it was called the "bush television" amongst the camping fraternity. Many a night, I had sat as darkness fell, gazing raptly into the flames of my campfire, the only illumination I had beside the moon and stars, listening to the covert rustlings of the night creatures in the surrounding undergrowth. The simple pleasure of a fire, a cup of coffee, and the beauty of the wild woods was all that I had needed. It used to be my idea of heaven, but heaven had fallen. How things change.

"It's a fact of life that things sometimes fall apart, but it's how we put them together again that really matters," said Sally.

She was sitting beside me; I hadn't heard her approach or been aware of her sitting down. She took my arm and nestled her head against my shoulder.

"I know you've never had a family, Adam. You've been used to dealing with things on your own, standing on your own two feet, self-reliant. But now, you don't have to, not anymore. You have a family now, and it's one worth keeping.

"Please don't turn away from us, Adam. Don't cut yourself off and try to go it alone. Grief needs healing, and it heals better if you have help."

Tears stung the back of my eyes. "It's hard, Sal," I murmured.

"It's hard for all of us," she said. "That's why we need to pull together, not give up. Jules wouldn't have wanted us to let his passing stop us from going forward. He wouldn't have ever given up and neither will we."

"But all our people, the children..." I said.

"Have made a decision and had decisions made for them by those who care. Being self-sufficient is one thing, looking after yourself, not relying on anyone, I understand that. But that time has passed now. Don't underestimate them, Adam. Give them credit for having their own minds about what they want and where they want to be. Any one of them could have left anytime they wanted; they still can. They have found something here that goes beyond just surviving. Have faith in that and put away all this self-doubt once and for all.

"Jules knew who you were as soon as he laid eyes on you. He knew what you were capable of. He believed in you and so do I and all the others. Let's stick to our original plan, take one day at a time, work together, and be a family."

"And Tina?" I asked. "Will she ever be part of our family again?"

Sally's face clouded over. "I honestly don't know," she said. "Tina only responds when the twins come to visit her. She's shut herself away in some private world and is not letting anyone in. I'm worried for her."

"We had a thing," I said. "I'm not sure what it was exactly, mutual comforting I guess."

"You think I didn't know?" Sally asked. "Tina and I often talked over a glass of Pinot Noir when the twins were asleep. You had a special place in her heart, but it wasn't anything more than that. You don't have to feel guilty about you and Linda."

"I don't... I think," I admitted, "but I can't help thinking, if we hadn't chosen that particular time to go to Thamesmead, if I had stayed behind..."

"It would have happened sooner or later. Kaminsky was just waiting for his chance; it was always going to happen."

"Maybe..." I said.

By the time Sally and I walked back, camp had already been set up. The mood was still a little subdued, except for the kids who were having a whale of a time running in and around the woodland, brandishing birch branches as would-be swords. I wished I could be like that again, the innocence of youth.

"You okay?" Linda asked, handing me a cup of steaming coffee.

"Yes, yes, I am," I said and meant it.

"We decided to stay here for the night, maybe tomorrow too," Charlie said from across the barbeque, a cup of tea in one hand and a sausage roll in the other. "It's been an age since the kids could let off steam in the woods. It'll do 'em good."

"It's a great idea," I agreed. "I think all of us could do with some down time."

"Jeff and me want to go look around Dunstable tomorrow. It's only a few miles up the road, and there might be something worth salvaging," said Alan.

"Good idea," I said. "Would you mind if I came too?"

"No prob," Alan said. "You looking for anything in particular?"

"Not really," I said. "If we're staying here for a while, I thought I'd just get the lay of the land, see what's out there."

The coffee was good, so was the sausage roll Charlie provided; I noticed he had started another. Sitting in a circle around the fire in quiet reminiscence, I found myself thinking about our next step. We still had a fair amount of stores, but as Julie had said, bacon and sausages were running low. Sausages we could make, but I didn't imagine for a second that we would find any bacon in Dunstable. Still, I could dream; maybe we would strike lucky.

Linda came and sat beside me. For once she wasn't wearing her leathers. Sporting a white T-shirt and a pair of grey jogging bottoms, she looked really comfortable. White slip-on pumps graced her feet.

"When you're ready," she said with a twinkle in her eye.

"Ready?" I said, puzzled.

"Got a surprise for you," she grinned. "Wanna see?"

Standing up, she offered me her hands. Curiosity piqued, I allowed her to lead me through the trees to a small clearing on the other side of the hill. A blue two-tone tent had been pitched beneath an aging birch tree, sheltered by a low hedgerow. Two camp chairs and a cool box had been positioned, and a small, unlit campfire was in front.

"Your idea, I presume?" I smiled.

"Absolutely," she said, "Though Tom and his boys set it up for me. There's more..."

A multi-coloured windbreaker, unnoticed in the gloom, had been staked out around the tree trunk, half circling the tree. From the lower branch, an inverted ten-gallon water container was suspended, but instead of a cap, there was a shower head.

"You've been busy," I said, noting the towel hanging from one of the windbreaker stakes.

"I thought you might appreciate a shower," Linda said. "Frankly, you could do with one..." She slapped a plastic soapbox into my hand and kissed me. "I'll start the fire."

It was heaven. The water was cool but not cold—refreshing in the humid heat. I washed the dirt and grime of a shitty week from my skin, liberally soaping myself down. With a sigh of pleasure, I opened the showerhead again and allowed the water to cascade over my body, sluicing away the soap and some of the hurt as well.

I felt great as I towel-dried my hair and scraped it back off my face with my fingers. Linda had left some sweats neatly folded on a box for me. There was even a pair of flip-flops, which made me smile for some reason. Where she had found flip-flops, God only knew.

"It feels good, doesn't it?" she said as I emerged from behind the tree.

"A million dollars," I said, accepting the cup of red wine and sitting in the camp chair.

"Couldn't run to get glasses," she said as we clinked the white china cups together and drank.

"No need," I said, taking a sip. "Mmmmm, good wine."

"Merlot," she informed me. "I figured red was better than white; there was no way to chill the Chardonnay."

I laughed. "You do realise we are at the back of beyond?"

"There's no wrong time or place for wine," she said.

"Not what I meant, but I take your point. Cheers, my darling!" We clinked cups again and drank.

"The service for Jules was lovely," Linda said after a minute or two of silence. "I wish I had known him better."

"He was a good man." I sighed. "He's going to be missed, but Sally put things into perspective for me. Whatever happens next, we will face it as a family. Jules will still have an impact on decisions, a good impact."

"To Jules," Linda said, raising her cup.

It had been a long time since I had spent any time in the woods. I was only amongst a few hundred trees in a blasted landscape, but it was a green oasis, and it was good. Thankfully the area was clear of vines and Creeps, maybe the fire sweeping across the landscape had something to do with it. I didn't know, nor did I care. The old feeling of peace and calm washed over me. I had the stars above me and the earth beneath my feet. It felt like home. It was home.

We lay head-to-head on a blanket beside the fire, our feet at opposite ends of the blanket, the warmth washing over us as we stared up at the night sky.

"Have you noticed how clear the sky is now, how bright the stars are?" Linda said.

"I have," I answered. "It's beautiful."

"Absolutely," she murmured.

Laying there was great; our silence was comfortable.

"Can you really navigate by the stars?" Linda asked suddenly.

The question came out of the blue and made me laugh. "Yes, I can."

"That's so cool."

"Not when the sky is full of clouds," I said, popping her romantic bubble.

"What do you do then, when the sky is full of clouds?" she persisted.

"Revert to basics," I said, "a map and a compass."

"That's cool too," she said.

"I can teach you if you like," I offered.

"You could?"

"Of course," I said. "You see that bright star there?" I pointed.

"The North Star," Linda said.

"Yes, Polaris, the only star in the sky that never moves, always stays in the north. And that one there, the three stars in a row, that's Orion's Belt. Those two constellations just to the left of Polaris are Ursus Major and Ursus Minor, the big bear and the little bear."

"And they tell you where you are and where you need to go?" she asked.

"Once you get to know their positions, yes," I said.

"What about a map and compass?"

"Easy to learn once you get the basics."

"I want to learn," she said earnestly, "but not right now..."

Is it inappropriate for me to think how lucky I am at this moment? The world is fighting for survival; the loss of life has been catastrophic. The future of my own people is uncertain in an uncertain land. We might never recover, and here I am, laying by a campfire with the woman I love, and I am happy.

Linda took my hand and gently led me to the tent. Inside, there was an air mattress, two pillows, a fitted sheet, and a lightweight sleeping bag spread like a duvet. Battery powered lamps, muted, gave the scene an intimate atmosphere.

Coming into my arms, Linda kissed me and her hand caressed my face. I crushed her to my chest, covering her face with fervent kisses. We were naked within seconds. Beneath the sleeping bag, we found each other, and at that moment I didn't care about the outside world.

Twelve

"Rise and shine, sleepyheads. It's a brand-new day!" Charlie sang over the radio.

I glared balefully at the radio nestled amongst the tangle of clothes on the floor of the tent. Linda stirred beside me.

"Drop your cocks and put on your socks. We got visitors," Charlie continued.

Linda came awake, laughing. "What did he say?"

"You heard right," I said, sitting up. "That's Charlie, subtle as a sledgehammer."

"You lovebirds reading me?" the radio persisted.

Linda's arm snaked around my waist and she held me close, her breasts pressing against my back.

"A few more minutes won't hurt..." she cooed.

"Lindy, believe me, there's nothing I'd like better, but if I don't answer, I guarantee you Mr. Sledgehammer will come through those tent flaps within the next three minutes."

Pouting, Linda fell back onto her pillow as I scrabbled for the radio.

"Morning, you arse," I said.

"Charming," Charlie returned jovially. "We can't all laze in bed, y'know?"

"And you make sure no one else does either."
I laughed. "What's up?"

"Breakfast, in the first instance," he said, "and we've got visitors."

"You said," I returned. "Is there a problem?"

"No, just thought you ought to know."

"Okay, we're on our way."

The Volkwagen Kombi stood out like a sore thumb against the white vans—a two-tone blue affair parked at the foot of the hill. There was a Ford Escort van sitting behind it. Charlie met us with a familiar twinkle in his eye.

"Don't start," I warned.

"Who? Me?" he said innocently, falling in beside us.

I didn't deign to comment.

Three of the five people sitting around the fire got to their feet as we approached. One of the two who remained seated was a boy, maybe ten or eleven. The other was a young blonde woman who looked totally out of place around a campfire. Despite the rough circumstances, she was immaculately turned out; her short hair didn't have a strand out of place, and her make-up was perfect right down to the sculptured lip gloss and her long, bright red nails. Her Nike trainers were pristine white, as was the delicate pink Nike tracksuit she wore. She sat, knees together, hands in her lap, pouting into the flames.

"Sean McCormick," said one of the three standing, his huge ham of a hand extended.

A big buff Irishman with a light Dublin accent and striking blue eyes, Sean had short grey hair cropped close to his enormous skull.

"And this is my wife, Maureen," he added as I took his hand and was engulfed by his massive fingers.

"Pleased to meet you," I said.

Maureen McCormick stood close to her husband—a stout round-faced woman with a friendly smile and shoulder length brown hair.

"This is our son, Brendan," she said, indicating the boy, who rose to stand with his parents.

"You came from the encampment?" I said.

"Yes," Sean answered. "Major Saunders took the majority of the refugees back along the M25 toward Norfolk. We decided we didn't want to go with the herd."

"Nor did we," said the other man. "Christopher Scott, Chris, and this is my partner, Harmony Quaid."

I felt Charlie stir beside me and gave him a warning glare as Harmony looked up and nodded a half-hearted greeting. She and Chris were a good match. He was tall, athletic, and well-tanned with light brown hair and brown eyes. He was dressed like a department store mannequin in clean blue jeans and an unblemished white T-shirt. Despite the heat, the man didn't seem to be perspiring, not even lightly.

"What happened back there?" Linda asked.

"It wasn't good," Sean replied. "We were camped on the outskirts and got out pretty fast. The army trucks loaded a lot of people who didn't have vehicles of their own, and the convoy headed east along the motorway.

"It was pretty orderly, considering. Some of them were panicking, and the soldiers did a good job of keeping order."

"Dozens of trucks got out in the first hour and a half," Chris took up the narrative. "We were situated deeper in the camp; I figure at least fifty percent got out before us. After that, I don't know. The M25 was really congested; things were almost at a standstill. I decided north was a better option."

"So, what can we do for you?" I asked.

The McCormicks looked at each other. "We were hoping you would let us join your group," said Sean.

"Us too," chipped in Chris.

I try not to judge a book by its cover, but I was already concerned about Chris and his girl-friend. He seemed very eager to ingratiate himself and that worried me. There was something off about the pair of them, but I couldn't quite put my finger on it.

"Have you eaten?" I asked.

"Just getting that sorted," Julie said.

"Okay, eat. I need to talk to the others, okay?"

"We can pull our weight; we're not looking for charity," Sean said suddenly.

"That's not my concern," I said. "We're a democracy, all decisions are joint, but as far as you joining us, I don't see a problem."

"We have food," Maureen said. "Sean, show them."

"That's really not necessary..." I began.

Sean went over to the Kombi and hauled out a large blue plastic crate. He dropped it on the ground in front of us and flipped open the lid. It was full of army field rations.

"I've got five more crates of the stuff," Sean said.

I looked at him.

"No, no," he said, hands raised, "it's not stolen. The soldiers took as much as they could, but there was still a ton of the stores left in the supply tents, and they told us to help ourselves."

"Okay, that's good," I said. "Have some coffee, eat something, and relax. We'll work it out."

As we walked away, Chris was suddenly beside me.

"Hey, look, we haven't got anything to offer, no food or supplies, but we can work."

I can't say I was surprised at his attitude; it was his partner's ability that I was a little skeptical about. I heard Jules' voice whisper in my ear, and I was prepared to give them the benefit of the doubt.

"Don't worry," I said. "We'll talk in a while."

Not looking too sure, he slowed. I could feel his eyes on me as I walked away, then he went back to his partner.

"Really? Harmony?" Nat said sarcastically.

"Can't judge a girl by her name," Julie said.

"Yeah, in this case, I think you can." Nat snorted. "She looks as if she just stepped off a catwalk."

"The question is," I said, "what do we do with them?"

"I think we all know the answer to that already," Sally said. "We can't turn them away."

"But can we trust them?" Nat asked. "I haven't got a problem with the McCormicks, but those other two..."

"We'll keep an eye on them and see how they shape up," I said.

"Those army rations will come in useful," said Charlie, "and Sean looks capable."

"His wife was a seamstress," Sally added. "That will be handy too."

It was obvious that the McCormicks were favoured—Chris and Harmony not so much. But as Sally pointed out, we couldn't really turn them away, as much as we would like to. I shrugged. Time would tell.

"So, it's decided," I said.

Everyone nodded.

"Let's give them a proper welcome then, shall we?"

It felt odd riding in the back of the cab while Alan drove. He'd offered me the wheel, but I declined, seeing as he enjoyed driving it so much. Jeff was next to him as we headed northwest toward Dunstable. The newcomers were more than happy and relieved when we officially welcomed them into the family. Although, it was obvious that Harmony Quaid wasn't so thrilled—pouting and looking very unhappy—but she said nothing. We left them to their celebrations while we went scavenging. We didn't have a particular shopping list in mind; we were just hoping for something good. Linda planned to come, but her bike developed some sort of mechanical problem, so she stayed behind with Roger to sort it out.

There had been some serious burning in the town; many of the houses on the outskirts had been gutted. It looked as if the townspeople

had tried to burn out the green, and the fire had gotten out of control. Approaching from the east, we saw extensive damage, empty shells that were once homes bordering deserted streets, but no vines. Many of the greens and play areas were scorched and lifeless.

"According to this," Jeff said, perusing a large map book of Great Britain Roads and Towns, "there's a few business parks up ahead."

Minutes later, we pulled in, parking amongst a dozen or so warehouses.

"This looks promising," said Alan.

It wasn't. Every warehouse had been ransacked months ago, leaving nothing of worth. We moved on toward the town centre and checked out two more business parks on the way—nothing.

"Seems like a bust," I said as we pulled out of yet another business park.

"Such a quitter," Jeff joked.

"Absolutely," agreed Alan. "Scavenging is an art that requires patience and tenacity. You just gotta keep looking."

I laughed, realizing I was dealing with the experts. "I defer to your greater knowledge," I said, giving a mock bow.

The town centre was wrecked—trash and filth everywhere. It seemed as if the place had been evacuated for some time. Then I remembered Williams telling me that most outlying towns and villages were the first to be overrun by the vines and how other larger towns had been cleared as a safety measure.

"It looks like a war zone," Alan said as we cruised slowly down a street called Vernon Place.

"They left in a hurry," said Jeff. "Keep going, Al. Just as the road bends to the left, there's a street on your right, Broadwalk. There's a mall down there, Quadrant."

Weaving in and out of the wreckage of the deserted town, we pulled up in front of a two-story red brick building. The blue stylised frontage sign declared it to be the "Quadrant Shopping Centre" with a white "Q" on a blue field being the leading motif. It was an open-fronted building with a walkway leading through the middle, red herringbone bricks underfoot, and a pavilion with an apex roof to protect shoppers from the elements. To the right of the entrance was a Burger King, and to the left was a Car Phone Warehouse. *I guess the bottom has fallen out of both businesses,* I thought wryly.

"You and Jeff can check out all the shops here," Alan said. "I'm going to check out a Poundland at the other end of the walkway."

"Do you think a Poundland is worth checking?" I asked.

Poundland was a chain of shops owned by a German company, Steinhoff. They sold general goods at ridiculously low prices—hence the name. Last I heard, before the black Dust, they were in financial trouble and were closing down.

"That's the thing," said Alan, "looters tend to go for the high-class shops. Places like Poundland often get overlooked. It's always worth a look."

"Okay, but keep in contact," I said.

Most of the shops had been pillaged, mainly for food and other comestibles. We came across a camping store. The windows were smashed,

and the inside was generally wrecked, but there were still a lot of goods we could use, mainly hardware, axes, knives, Laplander saws, tents, and tarps. We piled anything useful outside the store, including a lot of winter wear, parkas, and down jackets. I couldn't be sure what the weather in Scotland was going to be like, and I wanted to be prepared.

"Hey you two, I got a find," Alan's voice crackled over the radio.

"We have too. Where are you?" I replied.

"Southwest corner near the coffee shop."

"On our way."

Righting a shopping trolley that was lying on its side, we loaded our treasure and had to use a second trolley when the first one filled up. Leaving them at an intersection, we went to find Alan.

The pile of canned food and bottled water was considerable as we approached the Poundland store. Jeff stepped out of the doorway with another carton and placed it on the pile.

"Told ya," he grinned. "There's a ton of dry goods too."

"No bacon?" I said hopefully.

"Sorry," he said, "but even if there was, it wouldn't be safe to eat."

"I know," I said.

"We need to find a functioning deep freeze before we can trust any meats," Jeff said, "and there's little chance of that."

My optimism was crushed.

"I got this by way of compensation," Jeff said, indicating a carton of canned hotdogs.

"Hotdogs is not bacon ... or even sausages," I said sourly.

Gathering more shopping trolleys, we formed a train and took our plunder back to the cab, picking up the camping gear on the way. We managed to fit it all in, although sitting in the back suddenly became a bit of a feat. Dunstable had a lot more to offer, and Alan and Jeff were already planning another run tomorrow. I would leave them to it. I decided urban scavenging wasn't my forte. I think Alan and Jeff agreed, though they didn't actually say so.

Thirteen

I was still lamenting not finding any bacon as we drove back into camp and parked near the coach. The heated shouting reached my ears before I even got out of the cab and drove all thoughts of porcine delicacies out of my head. A group had gathered by the campfire where the ruckus was emanating. It took me a second to recognise Tricia's angry voice above the others. I had never seen or heard Tricia angry before, and her voice was filled with outrage.

Pushing through the crowd, I found Tricia facing off against Harmony Quaid over the unlit campfire; both women were red-faced and spitting flame. Oddly, the impeccable Harmony had a dirty face and mud down the front of her pink designer tracksuit top.

"I don't care what she did," Tricia said, barely keeping her rising temper under control.

Nat was standing to one side of her and apparently holding her back.

"You keep your hands off my children!" Tricia shouted.

"Your children?" spat Harmony. "She's a bloody *Chink!* How can she be yours? She needs to be taught some manners; look at the state of me!"

"You nasty bitch!" Tricia said, lunging forward.

Fortunately for Harmony, Nat was definitely holding Tricia back.

"She's a child! She was just trying to be friendly. There was no need to push her like that. No wonder she retaliated."

"Retaliated?" Harmony's voice rose an octave every time she opened her pink-lipped mouth. "The little brat threw mud at me!"

"You hurt me!" Wei Lin shouted. Joan held her protectively behind the arguing women. "I was just saying hello."

"Your hands were filthy, you disgusting, little…"

"That's enough!" I said, stepping out of the crowd. "What's going on?"

"Ask that old bag!" Harmony snarled, brushing down the front of her top.

I had to bite my tongue.

"First off, I think you ought to show a little respect," I said tightly. Harmony just glared.

"Trish?"

Breathing heavily, Tricia fought to control herself. "Wei Lin saw her sitting by the fire pit all alone and thought she looked sad, so she ran over and gave her a hug to cheer her up."

"With filthy hands!" Harmony interjected.

"Please…" I said to Harmony. "Go on, Tricia."

"Little Miss Cleanliness pushed Wei over, and the poor little mite grazed her knee. Wei Lin retaliated by throwing a handful of mud at her. Then Harmony grabbed Wei by the arm and began to shake her violently and shout abusively till I intervened."

"Is that what happened?" I said, turning back to Harmony.

She fidgeted, shifting from one foot to the other. "She needed to be taught a lesson."

"Not by you!" Tricia said, angry all over again.

"Okay, okay," I placated. "Tricia's right: no one lays a hand on the children. If you have a problem, you see Tricia or Joan. Secondly, we're talking about an eight-year-old child." I raised my eyebrows at her. "Really? I think apologies are in order."

Harmony looked mortified. "I'm the injured party here!" she whined.

"You're supposed to be an adult," I said.

Her face worked, desperate eyes settling on the gathered crowd, moving from one implacable face to the other. Her mouth writhed, but no sound came out.

Abruptly, Harmony whirled and stomped off.

"I swear, I'll swing for her," breathed Tricia.

"Hey, it's okay," Nat said, putting a comforting hand on her shoulder.

"Walking around here like the Queen of Sheba, sticking her nose up in the air..."

"Tricia," I said softly.

She turned to me questioningly.

"Remind me never to piss you off," I said.

She gawked at me, then burst out laughing.

Tricia turned to Wei Lin. "Come on, little one, let's go get that knee looked at. Maybe we can persuade Charlie to give you some sweeties."

The crowd dispersed, and Nat and I watched Tricia lead the little girl toward the coach.

"I'm not sure if Harmony Quaid is going to live up to her name," Nat said quietly so no one would overhear.

"We'll see," I said. "Where's Chris?"

"No idea," Nat said. "I haven't seen him all day."

Linda pulled up beside Roger, gunning the motorbike engine which roared healthily.

"Looks as if it's done the trick," she said.

"Just a little dirt in the fuel line," said Roger.

"You should be wearing a helmet riding that thing," I said. "And I thought it was supposed to be 'boys and their toys'?"

"Thought wrong, mate," Roger said. "Linda could give me a run for me money any day of the week when it comes to bikes."

"I don't doubt it," I said.

Memories of almost a year ago came to mind: the shy, almost newlywed lost in a storm of black Dust, frightened, alone. Then I look at the leather clad vision in front of me—smiling, happy, and confident. I couldn't help but think that at least something good came out of all this.

"Flattery will get you everywhere," Linda said cheerily.

"You missed a bit of a brouhaha earlier," I said, returning her smile.

She frowned when I told her about Harmony Quaid.

"I agree with you. There's something off about those two," Linda said.

"Other than the fact that they're walking fashion shows, you mean?"

"I don't really trust them," she answered.

"I'm a builder," Sean said. "Brick laying mainly, though I'm a bit of a Jack-of-all-trades; I can turn my hand to most things.

"Maureen is a seamstress; she could make a fashion statement out of potato sacks."

Sitting beside her husband, Maureen blushed.

"That's good to know," I said. "Both skills will be very useful in the time to come."

Sean beamed happily. "I'm sorry about earlier," he said. "Harmony was totally out of order. She shouldn't have spoken to you like that."

"Forget it," I said. "She's a big girl. You don't have to apologise for her."

"I know, but Maureen and I kind of feel responsible for bringing them here," Sean continued. "I don't want anyone thinking we're like that."

"Trust me. They don't," I reassured him. "Where are you from?"

"We lived in Kennington, South East London, but originally, we came from Ireland. Been here nearly twenty years, came over just after we were married."

"I know Kennington a little," I said. "How did you end up in the encampment at South Mimms?"

"The army evacuation put us in Hyde Park. Then when that got too crowded, they moved everyone with transport out to South Mimms. That was eight months ago," explained Sean.

"It wasn't bad at first, then water became a problem, and the army began bringing it in by tanker," Maureen said. "We had to wait hours in a queue just to fill one five-gallon container. We weren't allowed any more."

"It must have been rough," I said. "What about food?"

"Fresh food ran out pretty quickly too, then the canned stuff ran out. Finally, we were living on army K-rations; those bloody things never ran out!" snorted Sean.

"Come on, we were lucky to have them," Maureen chided good-naturedly. "It was the young ones I felt sorry for, no fresh milk, just some fortified white powder that had to be mixed with cold water; it tasted like chalk."

"And it was awful in tea," Sean added with a grimace.

"I take it leaving wasn't an option?" asked Charlie.

"And go where?" asked Sean. "We have the Kombi but no petrol except the small allowance the army gave us. We had no food except army rations, and they were still under strict rationing, no pun intended.

"It was only when we got the order to move this time that things changed. We were given everything we needed from the surplus supplies. But we have had enough of running with the herd, so we decided to head out on our own."

"We were going to go to Yorkshire, find somewhere in the Dales where the vines hadn't reached yet. We saw your bonfire and decided to come here," Maureen said.

Glances passed between Charlie and me, but we said nothing. It was obvious that the real danger of the vines had been withheld by the authorities, keeping people in the dark, including the McCormicks. It wasn't a good strategy.

"And you're welcome," I said.

"Chris and Harmony joined us as we reached the motorway," Sean said. "I didn't see any problem about travelling together..."

"We live and learn," I said.

Sitting in a circle around the campfire, we listened as Sean and Maureen told us their story. It sounded like so many stories we had heard several times before. Chris and Harmony were conspicuous by their absence.

"Where are they?" queried Linda. "Shouldn't they be here to hear our plans?"

"They were here for dinner," Julie said, "then they went back to their van."

"Let's not worry about it. I'll let them know what's been decided later," I said, standing up to address the others. "Tomorrow, we're leaving bright and early. Breakfast will be quick, so if you get up late, you'll miss it. Sean, you'll drop in behind the coach, and Chris can follow you. We haven't any more radios, so watch out for Charlie's signals."

"No problem," Sean agreed.

"There's no rush now; time's our own. But at the same time, I don't want to dawdle too much. We struck lucky in Dunstable regarding supplies. Alan and Jeff went back and got a second load, so provisions won't be an immediate problem."

"Especially if you like hotdogs," Alan quipped.

"Yeah, thanks for that, Alan," I said, pulling a sour face.

Everyone laughed.

"We'll scavenge more as we go," said Alan. "There's quite a few towns ahead, so if there's anything that's needed then, let me or Jeff know, and we'll see what we can do."

"We gave Jules a good send off," I said to Tina later that evening.

We were in the coach alone; everyone else was still around the campfire. The kids were playing nearby, burning off the last of the day's energy before settling down for the night. Tina was still unresponsive, having said nothing to me during my daily visits except for that first time. Sally told me again that Tina only reacted when the twins were there, but it was vague even then. Tina spoke to them as if they really were babies and not just something she called them.

"I'm going to miss him," I continued softly. "I miss you. I want the old Tina back; we all do. The happy, sparkling Tina who loved to tease, was quick to laugh and pleased to help.

"Time's all ours now, Tina; we have all the time in the world. We're going to get to Scotland and make a good life, all of us, and you need to be a part of that, part of us. The twins need their mum back. They're happy and well looked after, but no one can replace a mother's love, your love."

Tina shifted in her bed, but there still was no response.

"We're moving on tomorrow, no rush, just taking our time. A few newcomers joined us. The McCormick family, Sean and Maureen and their son, Brendan. Good people, you'd like them. I'm not too sure about the other two new-bies, Chris Scott and Harmony Quaid. She's a piece of work, and he disappears a lot. I'm not

sure they'll last. Even Tricia lost her temper with the girl, never seen that before!"

Leaning forward, I gently took Tina's hand in mine; it was warm and soft. She didn't resist or pull away this time, which I guess was something.

"Come back, Tina. You're safe now. I'll never let anyone or anything hurt you again, I promise. Just come back..."

She just lay there, eyes open, staring into whatever strange world she was lost in.

I let the last of the soft grey ashes slip through my fingers. They were immediately carried away by the soft breeze blowing around the green hilltop. Most of the funeral pyre was gone—wind-blown and scattered all over the tiny hill oasis. It made me smile; Jules had gotten his last wish, and I was glad.

"We're leaving now, Old Man," I said.

In my mind his voice echoed, *"Not so much of the 'old'..."*

"Give my love to Celeste. Tell her, from me, that you were a good friend, the best. I'll never forget what you did for me."

I scuffed the toe of my boot at the edge of the scorched circle as I looked out over the dark landscape—blackened and burned. The sun had been up for about an hour, stretching my shadow out behind me, lost among the shade between the trees. It was a good place to leave my friend. As I turned to walk down the hill, I knew that a part of me would always be here with him.

The camp was a hive of activity. Everything was packed, the fire was doused, and Tricia and Joan were herding the children onto the coach.

"Okay?" Linda asked, giving me a cup of coffee which was still warm.

I nodded. Linda always seemed to know my mood, never pressuring, just patiently waiting, happy to talk or just listen.

"I saw Chris this morning," she said. "He looked like shit; he said he was coming down with something. Anyway, I told him what was expected and left him to it."

"Thanks," I said.

"Hey," came a voice from behind.

"Bloody hell! You look like a bruised banana!" Linda exclaimed.

Pete Hogan blushed. The dark facial bruising had receded to a sickly yellow and purplish blue. His eye was still a little swollen, but the cuts and abrasions had scabbed over and were well on the way to healing. It was the first time I had actually seem him fully dressed and on his feet since leaving the Block.

"Yeah, but it's better than it was," he said. "Still hurts to laugh, but Sally said I should be okay to move around providing I don't overdo it. I can't handle staying in bed any longer."

"Just take things easy, one step at a time; we've got your back," I said.

"I feel pretty useless at the moment," he said. "Is there anything I can do?"

"And have Sally come down on us if you have a relapse? Not on your life! Just chill. Your time will come."

Pete laughed, then held his side. "Okay, I will," he said, groaning.

We were almost ready to roll when I saw Tricia walking back along the motorway, looking toward the hill where we laid Jules to rest. Something about her posture rang an alarm; her shoulders were hunched and her head bowed. I realised she was crying.

"Trish?" I said softly.

She glanced at me, then quickly turned away but not quick enough to hide her tears.

"What's wrong?" I asked.

Her sigh was heavy and full of sorrow.

"He's really gone, isn't he?" she said, her voice barely above a whisper.

"But he'll never be forgotten," I comforted.

"I won't ever forget him," she said, dabbing her eyes with a handkerchief.

She turned to me, and there was a strange look in her eyes, something deeper than the loss of a friend.

"Tricia?" I wondered.

"We spent time together," she said softly. "Not often, just when we needed comfort, to feel the loving touch of another human being, someone to ward of the darkness and the loneliness that surrounded us."

"I didn't know," I faltered, hoping she didn't see my surprised expression.

"No one did," Tricia said, looking back to the hill. "It's how we wanted it." She paused. "He was a special man, Adam."

"Very special," I said, taking her into my arms.

We stood quietly for a few moments.

"I was fine," she said into my shoulder. "I thought I had it under control. Then Susie Yarrow asked about him this morning, and it all came flooding back. It was awful what those poor mites went through when the black Dust fell. They were so afraid, but Jules made everything alright. He made them laugh, told them stories and tall tales like he always did."

"I never got the full story on how you ended up at the Block."

"Pure luck," Tricia said, stepping away. "A school trip was arranged to Mudchute Farm in the east end of London..."

"I know it," I said.

"Of course, taxi driver." Tricia managed a glimmer of a smile. "The kids loved it, the horses, the donkeys, they even had llamas. The petting section was a particular treat, even when the geese put up such a fuss.

"It was just me and another teacher, Jack Reynolds, and fourteen children. He drove the school bus to the farm."

She paused, and her face clouded as she relived the events.

"We were on our way home when the black Dust hit. It was light at first and didn't seem threatening. We thought it was ash from a big fire somewhere. We were diverted at the Blackwall Tunnel back along the A13 to the Rotherhithe Tunnel. There was a lot of traffic, and the Dust began to get heavier.

"Coming up through Greenwich, the bus started to act up, finally stalling just as we got to the junction of Greenwich Church Street. We weren't the only ones; cars were breaking down

all around us. Jack said the Dust was choking the engines' air intakes.

"Everyone just seemed to disappear, abandoning their cars, trying to find shelter. We shouted for help, but no one listened. Jack said it was probably best to stay with the bus, but the children were beginning to panic. The Dust was blotting out everything; we couldn't see a thing. We heard plenty though: cars colliding as stupid people whose cars hadn't broken down yet tried to drive through the blinding Dust, and people screaming, panicking, blundering around not knowing where they were or where they were going.

"I didn't think it was safe staying with the bus, and we needed to find shelter. Long story short, Jack very reluctantly got out of the bus to check some nearby shops. He found a burger bar, open but deserted. I shepherded the children inside before the Dust really began to fall." Tricia sighed heavily.

"I didn't think things could get any worse, but they did."

"What happened?" I asked.

Tricia sat on the guardrail at the edge of the motorway and looked up at the hill as if just seeing it brought comfort. Her face suddenly twisted in anger.

"He left us, Adam. Four days after the Dust stopped, the bastard told me to wait at the burger bar while he went for help. He said it was too dangerous to take the children out into the Dust, and there was a police station just down the road. I never saw him again."

"Damn," I said.

Closing her eyes, she slowly shook her head. "If I could have gotten my hands on him, I would have killed him," she said, "but I had the children to think of. I couldn't let them see I was scared. I kept telling them that help was on its way."

"What did you do?" I said, sitting on the guardrail beside her.

"The only thing I could think of was to walk back to Bexley and get to the school. But before I could get going, the Dust started to fall again. Thankfully, the burger bar had plenty of stores, though I have to admit, we were all getting a little bored with burgers and chicken nuggets. Then we lost power. I had to cook over a fire in a bucket. The children thought it was great!" Despite her anguish, Tricia laughed. "Kids!"

"It's surprising what they can deal with," I agreed.

"Well, the Dust finally stopped, but I was in a dilemma. I had no idea if the Dust would start again, and I didn't think it was a good idea to try to walk home. I went out and nearly choked when all the Dust kicked up, clouds of the stuff. Guiding fourteen children back to Bexley through this Dust that was lighter than air was crazy. We would have had to move so slowly, it would have taken hours.

"I decided to wait just a little bit longer. The children were fretting, some crying for their parents. There was only so much singing and playing 'I spy' a child can handle before boredom becomes an issue."

"So you stayed?" I asked.

"Yes."

"And got caught by the thunderstorm?" I asked, already knowing the answer.

"I should have tried for home when the Dust stopped," she said sadly.

"No, you did the right thing," I disagreed. "You were safe, you had shelter, and you had food. It was the right thing to do."

"Says the survival expert," Tricia smiled.

"I do," I answered. "So, the rain came and went and with it the Dust..."

"Yes," Tricia said. "I told the children we were going for a walk back to school, and that we would soon be home; they just needed to be brave for a little while longer."

Tricia paused again, her face strained, tears welling up in her eyes.

"I nearly took them through Greenwich Park, Adam," her voice cracked a little. "If it hadn't been for Nat..." she said, falling silent.

"Nat?" I said, confused.

"Yes," continued Tricia. "I figured the shortest way back was through the park. We could get to the main A2 and hopefully find help. Thank Heaven Nat found us. We were right there, right at the park gates, when I heard her screaming for me to stop.

"I didn't know, Adam. I didn't know the danger." Her tears flowed again.

Taking her in my arms, I hugged her.

"No one knew, Trish, until it was almost too late. The main thing is that you were safe, you brought the children home, and you've been amazing with them ever since."

"Nat brought us to the Block, and Jules took us in, looked after us. We were such a sight! Dirty,

God Alone knows what we smelt like, and we were so sick of burgers and chicken nuggets!"

That made us both smile.

"Nat got the addresses of all the children and risked her life over and over to find their parents. She managed to find all but six. It was then that I knew I was to be their guardian. There were lots of tears, but with Jules' help, we succeeded in calming the children and making them feel safe and wanted. The six became my children, *our* children. It broke my heart to see them pining for their families, and I knew it was a pain they would always have."

"You give them love, you care for them, and they know you wouldn't let anything happen to them. You should be proud of that."

"It felt a lot easier with Jules' encouragement. It's been hard these last few days."

"We're here for you, Tricia, all of us. You know that."

"I do," she agreed wanly. "And that's what's held me together, but this morning with Susie..." She sighed heavily. "It doesn't get any easier."

"It will," I assured her. "We're family."

I looked back toward camp.

"Come on, let's get back. They're ready to leave, and the kids need you."

"Adam," Tricia said, touching my arm, "about Jules and me..."

"I won't tell anyone," I promised.

Tricia smiled. "Thank you," she said, taking my arm.

Together, we walked back to the coach.

Fourteen

Three hours later, we passed Junction Thirteen on the M1. It was a beautiful day, clear sky, open road with the minimum of abandoned vehicles. It was still damned hot, but cool in the cab with the AC blasting. Linda and Roger were up ahead, and there was nothing to report. Alan and Jeff mentioned Milton Keynes, the country's first so-called New Town, was up ahead off Junction Fourteen and might be good pickings. Newport Pagnell Services was at Junction Fourteen. It would be a good place to stop for a while—maybe for the night. I knew it would make for a short day, but we weren't in a race.

"Adam, there's someone behind us," Jeff crackled on the radio.

"Can you see who?" I asked.

"Only that they look military."

The army? Again? It seems like we are running into these boys every time we turn around.

"Okay, let's just maintain speed and let them catch up; they're probably just heading north like us."

They weren't.

A few minutes later, I saw the two olive green vehicles in my side mirror, and the leader was flashing us down. Indicators flashed and the convoy slowed, not bothering to pull over to the side but stopping in the middle lane of the motorway.

A flash of white in my mirror made me look again as I cruised to a halt. Chris Scott's Escort van broke formation and accelerated along the near side lane. He wasn't speeding exactly, but he wasn't going slow either.

"What the hell?" I muttered.

I had no idea what he was doing or where he was going, and there was no way to stop him either, not that I was really bothered. I turned my attention to the approaching army vehicles, two of them, an armoured car leading and a small personnel carrier behind.

Getting out of the cab, I walked back to meet the officer as he dismounted from the armoured car.

"Is there a problem?" I asked.

"No, not at all," he said. "You're Adam Blake."

It was more of a statement than a question.

"I am," I said warily. "And you are?"

"Lieutenant Paulson. I'm under Major Saunders. He said I might run into your group along the M1."

I relaxed. "What can I do for you?"

"Nothing," said Paulson, "at least not directly; we're after some stolen supplies."

My stomach did a flip-flop. Glancing over at the Kombi, I saw Sean standing by the driver's door.

"Supplies?" I echoed. "What, food or weapons?"

"Medical," said Paulson. "The Red Cross Tent was burgled, and a large amount of

pharmaceuticals were stolen, some very dangerous narcotics.

"You haven't seen any strangers outside of your group on your travels by any chance? Maybe passing you, heading north?"

"No," I lied. "We..."

"I joined them two days ago." Sean suddenly appeared beside me. "All we took were field rations, with the Major's permission. If you want to search my van..."

"That won't be necessary," Paulson said amiably. "We were informed about the food rations. Whoever stole the medical supplies is probably long gone by now. We've got people looking at the main group and another splinter group that headed west. I very much doubt we'll find anything though. I'm sorry to have delayed you. I'll let you get on."

Some of the others had gathered around as Paulson returned to the armoured car.

"Wait."

Paulson turned.

"The evacuation, how did it go?" I was dreading the answer.

"Splendidly," he said. "No casualties. The bombs were pretty much confined to central London."

"That's great," I said, relief washing over me. "Really great."

Paulson smiled. "Frankly I'm not sure if it was good planning or just good luck, but it worked out in the end."

I nodded. I was glad the refugees had survived, but the realisation that London was gone hit hard. Now there was no going back. The way ahead might be uncertain, but only a burning ruin lay behind us.

"Well, I don't think there's any point in carrying on with my search, so I'll return to base." Paulson tipped his hat. "You and your people take care and good luck, Mr. Blake." Whirling his finger in the air to indicate they were turning back, the soldier headed for the armoured car.

Once on board, both vehicles U-turned and headed south.

"Bastard!" Charlie cursed. "That's why he shot off as soon as he saw the army trucks. Him and that stuck-up girlfriend of his."

"We don't know that for sure," I said.

"Like fuck we don't. Why did he piss off in such a hurry then?" Charlie said.

"When we find him, we'll ask him," I said. "Meanwhile, let's get to Newport Pagnell Services; I'm getting hungry."

I acted as if it didn't matter, but it did. As we drove on, I found myself thinking about Chris and Harmony—their strange behaviour, the clothes, their reluctance to mix with the rest of the group. They had an air of secrecy about them, or was it cunning? Their van was always locked, they were careful no one ever looked inside. Was it just a privacy thing or something more sinister? Charlie's question rolled around in my head. *Why did they leave? Was it the military? Or did they decide to go it alone?*

I sighed, realising I was wasting my time on unanswerable questions.

"Adam, do you read?" Linda's voice interrupted my thoughts.

"Go ahead, Lin."

"What's going on? Chris just went tearing past us like a bat out of hell."

"Not sure what's going on, Lin. Chris just suddenly took off, no reason, no explanation. Where are you?" I added.

"Just left the Services, looks okay. We're on our way back to you."

The green and white signage fixed to the side of the walkway spanning the motorway proclaimed "Welcome Break," a franchise that ran motorway services such as Newport Pagnell, one of thousands across the country. If memory served me right, Newport was bigger than most with all the usual concessions: Starbucks, W.H. Smith's, Subway, Burger King, KFC, and the notable addition of Harry Ramsden's Fish and Chips—a rarity in Motorway Services. Just thinking about it made me long for some fish and chips with salt and lots of vinegar. I pushed the thought from my mind; it didn't do any good torturing myself.

As I approached the main parking lot of the services, I saw Alan and Jeff veer off toward the petrol station, forever on the hunt for fuel. The rest of the convoy pulled up in front of the main entrance to the food halls.

"I'm not sure what the condition the toilets will be in, but I've got a busload of desperate kids here," said Tricia as she disembarked off the bus.

"Okay, I'll get them checked out. Meanwhile, keep everyone in this area," I said.

Tricia, Joan, and Sally herded the children beneath the sheltering glass canopy on the front of the building which provided much needed shade. Moans and groans expressing the need to pee circulated among them. I got Charlie, Nat, and Sean and we headed inside.

It smelled musty from the dirt and refuse everywhere, but there was an overlying aroma that was sweet and sickly—one I recognised.

"Jeez, I'm never going to get used to creepy, abandoned buildings," Charlie said.

Coming out into the food hall, we clicked on flashlights. Despite being early afternoon with bright sunshine outside, we entered a room of deep shadows which danced on our peripheral vision. It was like a dozen places we had seen before: piled up rubbish, thick greasy dirt smothering the tiled floors, empty counters, and rotting food—the origin of the sweet sickly smell.

"The toilets are over there," said Sean, highlighting the sign with his flashlight.

Moving through the tables, we headed in the direction the sign indicated. Nat paused, her flashlight trailing across the floor.

"Nat?" I queried.

Curiosity piqued, I went over to her as she crouched by one of the tables.

"These are recent," she said, her torch beam indicating the scuff marks running across the dirty floor

The marks disappeared into the darkness.

"It looks like there were three of them: a man, a woman or maybe an older kid, and definitely a young child," Nat said.

"Impressive," I said.

"You live, you learn," she said, rising. "And I had a good teacher." Nat smiled at me. "I thought it might have been Chris and Harmony but not with a child."

"I agree," I said. "Let's keep our eyes open."

"The toilets are okay," Charlie called across the room. "A bit pungent but clean enough. There's even running water, though I wouldn't recommend drinking it."

"Let Tricia know. We'll carry on and search the place," I said.

Except for a case of tomato ketchup, large catering size, there was nothing to salvage from the kitchens or anywhere else. An open carton of mustard sachets was under the counter at Burger King. There were plenty of condiments but no burgers to go with them. We took what there was. It was strange how a place once so vibrant and rocking with life was now so eerie and silent—a dead place, full of ghosts and dust devils. It was depressing. I had to get outside.

Alan and Jess had returned, also empty-handed. I wondered at Jeff's odd expression as he stood wiping some dirt from his hands with a rag, constantly looking across the vast expanse of concrete surrounding us, frowning. The petrol station was on the farther side—eerily empty, quiet, and devoid of any visible life. Maintenance buildings dotted the area along with a few abandoned vehicles slowly baking in the hot sun.

"We've been to a lot of places just like this one," said Jeff, "but this place is different somehow."

"Different?" I queried.

"Yeah," he said. "We normally find something, not always of use, but something. Here, everything's been picked clean; there's nothing at all."

"Does it matter?" asked Charlie.

"Probably not," said Jeff. "It just felt odd somehow."

"Maybe you're losing your touch!" laughed Charlie.

"You better hope not," Jeff laughed too, "or we'll all be fucked!"

Standing in the sunshine was actually pleasant after the dim interior, but it wasn't a very agreeable view. The entire area was a wasteland—bleak, grey, lifeless, devastated by fire and the constant blistering sun. Over the back, on the farther side of the huge car park, clumps of vines ran rampant. There was a small woodland beyond the vines. Deep shadows enshrouded the branches and wooded floor. It was impossible to see if any Creeps lurked in the branches or if hostile eyes observed us, though it was highly probable. The thought made me shudder, echoing memories of the attack on Williams' encampment.

Did the Creeps strip the concessions bare? I didn't think so. They would have totally wrecked the place, and scavenging isn't what they did. I rethought my decision about spending the night here. I agreed with Jeff: the place didn't feel right.

"This place is torture," Charlie said, joining me by the coach. Linda was right behind him. "KFC, Burger King, Starbucks ... bloody apocalypse!"

I laughed. "Yeah, glad to see you got your priorities in order, but you missed Harry Ramsden's."

"Ah man! Fish and chips," lamented Charlie.

Sunlight glittered off the dirty plate glass sidings of the low flat buildings as I looked out over the car park once again.

"What is it?" Linda asked.

I looked at her, realising she was almost able to read my thoughts and know my moods.

"Sorry?" I asked disingenuously.

"You've got that look in your eye," she said, quickly kissing me. "Something's bothering you."

"It's probably nothing. It's just that this place feels off kilter; it doesn't feel right," I confessed.

"Jeff said the same earlier," said Charlie, forever eavesdropping.

"And I think we should take note," I answered.

"There's a place farther on; it's just open ground, no trees or bushes, no buildings. Looks like an old factory site, just concrete foundations," said Linda.

"We'll go there as soon as everyone's ready," I said.

It was like we cursed ourselves as Julie's stressed voice reached our ears.

"Charlie! Adam!"

She was at the farther end of the coach, pointing across the car park. She was holding Juney protectively in her arms.

"What's up, love?" Charlie called as I moved round the front of the coach.

Two trucks idled on the farther side of the car park—a red battered Transit and a small flatbed Volkswagen. I couldn't see the occupants.

"What do you suppose they want?" asked Charlie beside me.

"No idea," I said, "but let's not wait to find out. Something tells me it's nothing good."

"Should we go over there? They might need help," Roger said.

"If they needed help, they would be over here," I said.

"I could walk over and see what they want," suggested Charlie.

"No, we'll just go. Get everyone together. I'll keep an eye on them."

Everyone hustled onto the coach. It was barely half-loaded when the air was split by the roar of powerful engines. White exhaust fumes plumed into the air and tyres screeched as the two trucks hauled round in a tight circle and disappeared behind a low building.

"Want us to go check?" Linda asked, standing astride her motorbike.

"No, it feels all wrong. We keep together until we get back on the road. I'll lead."

Both Linda and Charlie frowned, probably because they thought I was overreacting. Maybe I was, but my instincts were going crazy with the overwhelming need to get away from this place. I led off slowly, my eyes scanning the landscape. Roger and Linda rode either side of me like wingmen. Alan was close behind in the van, and the others followed in tight formation.

Linda stood up on the bike's stirrups, craning her neck to see ahead. She drew slightly away from me and was shadowed by Roger.

"Shit! The exit's been blocked!" Linda cursed over the radio.

A few seconds later, I saw that the entire exit road had been barricaded with traction engines, squatting across the roadway like huge metal beasts—dead and baking in the sun. There was no way past them; a bicycle wouldn't get through.

"Rog, Linda, keep back," I warned.

Men suddenly appeared amongst the traction engines—hard looking men carrying clubs, hammers, and crowbars. I veered away as a shower of metal hurtled toward the cab, bouncing off the bonnet and rear door. A small hammer smashed through the rear side window with a loud bang, and the crashing of tempered glass startled me.

From behind the low building roared a fleet of small trucks—the red Transit and flatbed Volkswagen among them. The cabs were full of men as the vehicles raced to cut me off and encircle the coach. Linda and Roger shot away, circling the coach to keep the trucks away even as Charlie began to slow down. I snatched up the mike.

"Charlie, keep going! Turn around and don't stop for anything!"

Something heavy bounced onto the roof of the cab. I saw a brick fly off to the left from the corner of my eye. Something else clattered along the length of the cab from underneath; missiles rained all around me.

"Fuck this," I swore in a low voice.

The cab screeched to a halt as I slammed on the brakes and leapt out. Raising my Glock, I took quick aim and shot out the windscreens of three of the traction engines. The noise of gunfire and shattering glass was loud, and the men scattered.

The lighter trucks and vans were circling the coach, trying to force it to stop like red

Indians around a wagon train. I aimed at the nearest van and put three slugs through its rear panel. The bullets *spanged* loudly through the thin metal; it must have been like being inside a kettle drum. The van sheered away erratically.

The red transit broke out of the circling vehicles and headed toward me. I stood my ground and took aim, reluctant to fire into the crowded cab. Linda appeared beside the speeding van, firing repeatedly into the vehicle's engine compartment as she rode past. Smoke and steam billowed out, and the short bonnet popped open, blinding the driver. The smell of burning oil filled the air as the van lurched away from me, the engine grinding and clanking in its death throes.

The van doors flew open, and three men spilled out; one stumbled, fell, and rolled on the concrete. Roger tore past them, revving the motorbike and firing into the air. All three men scrambled for the cover of the traction engines.

"What do we do?" Charlie asked desperately over the radio.

Leaning into the cab, I grabbed the mike. "Head out the same way we came in."

The flash of green alerted me at the last minute, and I threw myself backward out of the cab. The crowbar punched through the side window, showering the interior with glass beads and landed in the passenger seat. The thug in the green jacket hauled the crowbar back out of the window and came round the rear of the cab after me. Grinning, showing yellowed teeth, he raised the crowbar threateningly.

"Really?" I said, firing into the air.

He stopped in his tracks and the crowbar clattered to the ground. I pointed the gun at him, and the blood drained from his dirty, unshaven face as he raised his hands in a gesture of surrender.

"Fuck off!" I said.

He turned and ran.

The others had made it to the entrance access road. The remaining vehicles that were harassing them fell back; the threat of our guns finally made them see sense. Two of the vehicles, a grey Nissan and some foreign job I didn't recognise, came barrelling toward me—not that the make of car made any difference when it came to running me down.

"Shit..." I cursed, moving away from the cab, fearing if I took cover behind it, they would simply smash into it.

The foreign job was bigger, so I emptied my Glock into the engine compartment and was rewarded with a satisfying banging and clashing as the engine blew, and the truck grinded to a halt. The Nissan accelerated as I reached for a second magazine. As fast as I was, I knew I wasn't going to be fast enough.

Glaring through the windscreen, the driver's eyes bulged as he gripped the steering wheel tightly. His mouth was wide open, though I couldn't hear him screaming over the protesting roar of the engine as he floored the accelerator. I tensed; it was going to be close. I feinted right then threw myself to the left a split second too late. The rear of the Nissan spun around, tyres screaming. I grunted as the bumper clipped my lower legs, flipping me into the air. I extended my left arm to break my fall as I hit the ground and rolling, and pain shot up to my shoulder.

Regaining my feet, I frantically searched for the Nissan. It turned in a tight curve, the tyres skidding on the rough concrete as the gears crunched and the wheels bounced, fighting to gain traction.

Keeping my eyes on the speeding vehicle, I shucked the empty magazine from the Glock and slammed in a full one. Even as I aimed at the vehicle's grill, I knew I was too late; its momentum was too great, and it would slam into me before my bullets stopped it.

The white transit braked directly in front of me. I had a brief glimpse of Alan levelling an automatic pistol at the Nissan and firing several short bursts. The Nissan swerved and tore off without slowing back toward the low buildings it had emerged from. Alan leapt from the cab and sprayed a quick burst after the fleeing vehicle.

"You okay?" he called over, grinning.

"I am now," I said, holstering my gun.

"I've always wanted to do something like that," he said exuberantly. "Blame Arnie!"

"I'm sure Mr. Schwarzenegger would be proud of you." I laughed.

I allowed Alan to precede me as we drove out of the services, keeping a close watch on my rear-view mirror. Only now, I felt the sharp stinging pain on my arm from losing several inches of skin to the rough concrete.

"Shit, that's going to hurt tomorrow," I muttered.

The coach was well ahead as we came onto the motorway. Sean's Kombi and Jeff's Transit

idled in the middle of the road, flanked by the two motorbikes. I flashed my headlights, and they pulled around and made off after the coach.

I pulled up beside Linda.

"Well, that answers that question," she said, leaning in and kissing me through the window. "Scavengers. They must have a camp nearby."

"Yeah," I said

"You alright?" She nodded at my bloodied forearm.

"Stings like fuck, but yeah, I'm okay," I said.

She shook her head at me, kicked the bike into gear, and I followed after her.

Fourteen

Fifteen

"Ouch!" I said.

"Stop being a wuss," Sally said, holding my arm tighter. "It's full of dirt and grit; it'll get infected if I don't clean it out." She dabbed the wound with a cotton ball soaked in surgical alcohol. It was cold on my skin and stung like a bitch.

"Didn't expect that," said Roger, watching Sally's administrations. "I don't know how we missed the blockade."

"Because no one expected it," Charlie said. "I'm guessing we're going to see a lot more of the same as time goes on."

"They were scavengers; that's why the services were picked clean," Nat said. "Judging by the tracks I found in the food hall, there must be a whole community around here somewhere."

"I'm surprised they don't have guns," Roger said. "It could have turned really nasty if they had even a shotgun or two. Although, I have to say I'm glad the fuckers didn't."

It was odd to hear Roger swear; he was a quiet man, not often given to displays of emotion or outrage.

"They probably have guns," I said as Sally dressed my arm, "just no ammunition. I'd bet they used it all hunting for food."

"Roger and I will pay closer attention in future, check out the areas we pass through more thoroughly. We should have spotted those barricades," said Linda.

"Like I said," reiterated Charlie, "it wasn't anyone's fault. No one expected a trap, and we'll know better next time."

"How were the kids?" I asked. "Any of them get scared?"

"No," answered Julie. "Tricia kept them distracted, so they didn't even know what was happening. A couple wondered about the gunfire, but we told them it was just one of the vans backfiring."

"I've got Jeff and Alan keeping watch in case those buggers try a sneak attack," Charlie said. "Though after having a taste of our guns, I don't think that's likely."

"Better safe than sorry," I said. "We need to set up a rota and watch through the night just to be sure. We should rethink our security as well, tighten it up, and make everyone more aware of our surroundings."

"There," said Sally. "Done. See me tomorrow and I'll change the dressing."

"Thanks Sal, you're a diamond," I said, flexing my arm. It felt good.

The area was as Linda said: a wide, empty expanse of concrete, no buildings, no foliage, with an excellent view all around the surrounding countryside. It was a couple of hours until nightfall, so we made camp and started the evening meal. It gave the children another opportunity to let off steam and the adults time to relax.

Tom Taylor's three boys produced footballs from somewhere, and an impromptu football game was in progress; from where I was standing, it was more like a melee as they ran about screaming and squealing in delight. A couple of the adults stood nearby, cheering them on with whistles and shouts of encouragement. I sensed it was only a diversion—a way to get over the shock of the day's events. Several of the family were shocked—adults as well as children—as the seriousness of our situation finally began to dawn on them. It was a real taste of what the world had become—a place of sudden violence. We had moved away from peaceful tranquillity with this life or death confrontation, and it made them see that the Derek Kaminsky incident was a mere appetizer.

"I feel bad," Linda said quietly.

"Why?" I asked.

We were seated in a couple of camp chairs in the shadow of the cab having a brief respite from the burning sun, drinking coffee.

"You could have been hurt or worse," she said. "I messed up."

"Bullshit," I said. "You saved me."

"It was Alan who did the saving." She smiled weakly.

"Lindy, it's likely to get worse. There's no way to know what lies ahead, and that's why I'm not rushing up to Scotland. We could be there in a day or two, but not knowing the conditions, I want to take it slower, give everyone a chance to come to terms with their new home.

"All we can do is watch each other's backs, keep each other safe, and we're already doing that."

Her eyes were troubled as she slipped her hand over mine. "I couldn't bear losing you," Linda said softly.

The next two days were uneventful as we pushed north. Alan and Jeff were having no luck scavenging the local towns we passed, and supplies were beginning to run low again. Leicester had been the first big city we encountered, but the approach was completely overgrown with vines. Spotting some activity in the trees crowding the roadside, Alan decided it was too dangerous to go any farther, and he and Jeff reluctantly turned around.

Nottingham, of Robin Hood fame, was the next city just to the east. We were confident it would produce the much needed supplies. To make sure, we also looked at Derby, a smaller city to the west along the A52.

"What do you think?" Charlie said, looking at the map spread out on the camp table.

"We should go for it," said Nat. "The more irons in the fire the better."

"I agree," Alan said.

I perused the map a bit longer. Both places were about the same distance from the motorway, and both had a good chance of giving us provisions.

"Two teams," I said. "Me, Charlie, Linda on the bike, Nat, and..." I glanced at Tom Taylor, "Andrew, if that's okay, Tom?"

"He's his own man," Tom said. "He doesn't need my permission."

Andrew was grinning from ear to ear.

"Okay, second team will be Alan, Jeff, Tom, and Roger. First team, Nottingham, second team, Derby."

I looked around the table. "Any questions?"

There weren't any.

"We'll empty the two vans, there's room on the coach now, and we'll transfer the stuff from one van onto there. We'll leave the Gennies under a tarp till later, though I want Alan and Jeff to take one to Derby in case you find fuel."

"We keep close contact via radio and no unnecessary chances. In and out. Find what we can quickly and meet back here at three."

Pete Hogan was on the side-lines as the meeting broke up. He looked good; the swelling had gone from his face with no signs of bruising. He still favoured his side but was otherwise recovered from the brutal beating he had received from Derek Kaminsky.

"I'd like to come with you," he said.

"Not this time. Give it a couple more days. I need you here to oversee Terry and the two Taylor boys; Sean will help. It's going to be your job to keep our people safe while we're away."

Pete looked glum but accepted the responsibility with good grace.

"I'd suggest you put someone on top of the coach as a lookout; Terry and Teresa to start, then have Paul and Stephen spell them, make sure they keep alert."

"I will," said Pete. "I'll have a go myself, so I don't feel so much like a spare part."

I laughed. "Your time will come. We still got a lot to do."

The Nottingham exit boasted a covered walkway which spanned the entire motorway, exit and entrance ramps included, something that was pretty unusual for service stations. We drove beneath the archway and headed into the city. There was some green on both sides of the road and plenty of undergrowth interlaced with young vines. Thankfully, they were too sparse to be of any real danger unless one got careless. The houses were mainly red brick, semi-detached, and all were empty. The unusual road signs caught my eye; they were round on single poles rather than the normal rectangle. Andrew was driving, relishing the task with a big grin on his face. I rode shotgun with Nat while Charlie lounged in the back. Linda rode scout.

Signs pointed the way to the town centre. Andrew followed Linda down the deserted streets of a modern day ghost town—streets totally devoid of life. Evidence of a hurried evacuation were everywhere: front doors left ajar, plastic bags of discarded clothes, even a few suitcases littered the pavements, remnants of a panicking populace. We diverted a couple of times, avoiding blocked roads jammed up with vehicles until we finally reached our destination.

"According to the map there are several retail parks dotted about here. Victoria, The

Exchange, Riverside, and various others. The first three are closest together; maybe we should check them out first," said Nat.

"That's a lot of ground to cover," said Charlie.

I studied the map. "No, Nat's right. We'll concentrate on these three. We can always come back if the pickings are good. We can search alone but keep within earshot of each other, and don't take any risks."

The retail park was like the city—deserted— with the same litter and crap everywhere, mainly windblown paper or plastic bags. The inevitable overturned shopping trolley laid like a stricken metallic beast in the gutter; others were strewn in various points throughout the estate.

All the shops were dark, but amazingly, their front windows were intact for the most part. Marks and Spencer and T.K. Maxx were among them, but Charlie and Andrew made a beeline toward the large Halfords outlet. Linda and I headed toward Argos while Nat set off to explore Morrison's.

"Just look. Make notes or leave markers. We meet back here in thirty minutes," I said.

I forced the glass doors open past the debris; large Argos catalogues had tumbled from a display next to the doorway and blocked it. With a crunching and grinding, the door squealed open. Linda helped as I put my weight against the toughened glass portal. Clicking on our flashlights, we entered warily.

"It's a black as Fingal's Cave in here," said Linda as we removed our sunglasses.

The shelves were fully stocked with electrical goods, toys, and gardening tools; a myriad of other household items were highlighted by the white glare of our torch beams.

"That's a good sign," said Linda.

"Let's check the warehouse," I said, moving behind the glass counters.

Linda followed me through a pair of rubber doors into the dark cavern beyond. Our footsteps were silent on the industrial flooring beneath our feet. Our flashlights swept the warehouse like a pair of miniature searchlights.

Storage racks standing twenty-five feet high marched into the darkness—mostly filled with beige cartons or shrink-wrapped goods on pallets. A red and yellow forklift sat uselessly in the farthest corner. Keeping next to each other, we made our way down the aisles one-by-one.

"These will be handy," I said, holding up a dark coloured box.

"Walkie-talkies," Linda said.

I read the technical specs printed on the side of the box by the light of the torch.

"Motorola Extreme, T82, six-mile range, sixteen channels, eighteen-hour battery life, charging pods." I gave a box the Linda. "They're perfect for our needs, and there's plenty of them."

"What about these?" Linda said, pointing out miniature security cameras on the next shelf.

"They'll be handy when we get to where we're going," I said, taking one of the boxes down and examining it. "Easy to install as well."

There were digital devices of all kinds: cameras, drones, and communications. All would be useful when we settled in Scotland. *If we settled in Scotland.* I pushed the dark thought away. There was a rack of batteries of all different sizes at the end of the aisle. I grabbed a selection and stashed them into my backpack. Another twenty minutes of searching didn't produce anything of use, so we headed back to the others.

"What the hell...?" Linda gasped as we went back out into the bright sunshine.

Charlie and Andrew were manhandling a huge square trailer across the car park, their faces red and sweating.

"Hey!" Charlie beamed at us. "Look what we've found! There's a ton of stuff back there in Halfords; this will help transport it."

Linda and I helped push the trailer over to the van.

"All the vans have trailer bars, even Sean's Kombi," said Andrew. "And there's more trailers back there if we need them. It'll give us a greater storage capacity without compromising people's space."

"That's a good idea," I said. "We found a lot of tech stuff which will come in handy too. But right now, I think we should concentrate on food and water. Let's go see what Nat's found."

It was a bonanza. The stench of rotting meat and fish aside, the giant grocery store was a goldmine: canned goods, dry goods, pasta, rice, tons of it. Some had been ravaged by rats or mice, but the vast majority was untouched.

"Finally, some good luck," Nat said.

I told Nat about Charlie's and Andrew's trailer.

We left the girls to hitch up the trailer and bring the van closer to Morrison's main doors, and Charlie, Andrew, and I began stacking

cartons of food. Soon the trailer and the van were loaded to capacity.

"We'll come back for the rest, bring the other vans, and then take the trailers," I said, wiping my face clear of sweat with the front of my T-shirt.

"Do you think the others had the same sort of luck?" Charlie asked.

"Even if it's only half as good as us, we've got it made," said Andrew.

"You're right," said Charlie, reaching into the van. "So, I reckon we've earned these."

We crowded around, each taking a beer. It was warm, but beggars can't be choosers. Sitting on a bench in the sunshine in the middle of a deserted town, drinking and laughing with friends was priceless; I was glad that fortune smiled on us again.

Linda pulled over to the side of the road and stopped. She pulled off her crash helmet, and shading her eyes, peered across a small field bordering the highway. Andy pulled up beside her.

"What's wrong?" I asked through the passenger window.

"I saw something moving over there near that long building, just a flash, like sunlight on glass or maybe metal."

I scanned the area with my binoculars. It looked like a small farmstead, a cluster of low buildings huddled together.

"There's something definitely moving over there," I said, "but I can't make it out."

"Creeps?" ventured Charlie.

"No," Nat said, using her own binoculars. "I think it's a dog; I can hear barking."

"Your ears are better than mine then," I said. I couldn't hear a thing.

"It's faint, but I'm sure I can hear it," Nat said.

"We should go look," Linda said.

I pondered for a moment. There was no obvious road leading to the farm, which meant we would have to trek across the overgrown fields of coarse, dry grass. There was no sign of tangled undergrowth or bushes, but that was no guarantee.

"Adam?" queried Nat.

"Maybe," I said slowly. "I'm not liking those trees over there; they're too damn close."

"We'll get in and out fast, no hanging about," Linda said. "I really think we need to go and check it out. It just feels ... necessary."

I looked at her; she was determined. "You and those bloody feelings of yours; you're worse than me," I said. "Okay, single-file. Keep close and watch those trees. The slightest sign of danger, we run for the van."

We went over the barrier bordering the road and made our way across the field. The grass was knee high and very dry. It scraped against my jeans like thin, bony fingers and crunched underfoot with brittle ease. The sun was merciless after the cool interior of the van.

"Move right," I cautioned, pointing to a patch of vines camouflaged among the undergrowth.

The vines were young, growing in small clumps within the field, and almost impossible to see from a distance—with or without binoculars. They didn't seem sentient right

now—guessing that would come. Remembering Melissa Baxter, I didn't want to risk the venom.

Taking the lead, I loosened my Glock as the dog's barking was clearly audible now—an excited, frantic yapping, shrill, insistent. Nat and Linda pushed forward. Nat had already unslung her bow and notched an arrow. Weapons drawn, we climbed the fence separating the field from the farm. The ramshackle buildings were totally derelict: sides sagging and roofs caved in. Doors hung askew on rusty hinges or had totally fallen off and lay rotting on the hard-baked ground.

Passing cautiously between the buildings, we edged into a farmyard that gave way to a wide area of open ground, surrounded by more buildings. A farmhouse sat on the farther side; the windows were dark and vacant; the slate roof sagged, and the yellow brick chimney had collapsed onto the other side of the house. Farm implements were strewn everywhere, broken and rusting in the sun. By the gate, parked close to a decrepit barn a small John Deere tractor sat forlorn, covered with thick mud and grease.

From this angle, I could see the stand of trees across the next field was more than a small copse as I had first thought. Like green uniformed soldiers, the trees marched off into the distance; it was a good-sized wood, bordering on being a forest. It made me feel even more uneasy, looking at the shadows beneath the boughs, wondering if hostile eyes were watching us.

"Holy shit..." Charlie said as we rounded the corner of the farmhouse

The fenced in garden was overgrown; weeds interlaced with more vines abounded, hissing and swaying on serpentine stalks amidst the sprawling undergrowth. There was a small outhouse—practically razed to the ground—and a dry-stone wall on the garden's western boundary. It was the Creep enmeshed in the rusting tangle of barbed wire dumped in the corner of the garden that made Charlie swear. The creature glared balefully at us as we gathered at the edge of the garden, its scabrous flesh torn and slashed by the vicious barbs, its matted fur glistening with dark, brackish blood.

The brute reared up, roaring noiselessly as we approached, seemingly oblivious to the fresh lacerations gouging across its flesh as it pulled against the restraining wire. Long, muscular arms lashed the air, and its bullet head thrashed as it struggled futilely to break free to get at us in its frenzied madness. Realising it was hopeless, the Creep remained standing, straining against the restraining wire, continuing to glare at us silently. I felt something slither across the surface of my brain—a repulsive skittering and a faint echo of crazed screaming made me shudder. Shaking my head, I drove the abhorrent sensation away.

The black and white Border Collie raced back and forth in front of the trapped Creep, barking and yelping loudly. The Collie looked exhausted; its long fur was matted with mud, and there was blood on its white socked feet. Its tongue lolled from its mouth—white and dry. Foam flecked its jowls, but it wasn't slowing down. It didn't stop its repetitive racing up and down in front of the enmeshed monster, even though we had happened on the scene.

"Easy, boy, easy," said Charlie, stepping forward and raising his Glock.

He took aim at the Creep, who sat back on its haunches totally unperturbed as certain death loomed, mere seconds away.

I looked at the dog racing back and forth, then at the trees. Alarms bells were sounding through the miasma of conflicting sensations flitting like angry bees in my head.

"Charlie, wait," I said.

Charlie hesitated, following my gaze toward the distant trees.

"If there's one, there will be others," I said.

"Then why aren't they attracted by his barking?" Charlie asked.

"I don't know," I said, "but let's not take chances."

Nat took her bow and notched an arrow. Taking quick aim, she sent the Creep to oblivion with an arrow through its heart. But the dog didn't stop barking. It just changed direction and ran in circles in front of the fallen outhouse.

"What the hell's the matter with it?" asked Andrew,

I dropped to one knee. I always had an affinity with animals—more so than people some might say. I was hoping that would come into play now as I tried to calm the frantic animal.

"Hey boy, come on, it's okay. Come on, it's gone, you're safe."

The dog ignored me, continuing its raucous racing, bouncing off the door of the outhouse laying askew on a pile of dirt, rushing back to me and then back to the door.

Nat moved closer to the wreckage.

"Listen, can you hear that?" she asked, cocking her head to one side.

Charlie stood beside her.

"That's a baby crying..." he said, almost in awe. "It's over there somewhere."

The dog became even more excited, running around in circles as we passed the outhouse and converged on a pile of debris beyond. Dashing past us, the dog stopped by a sheet of corrugated iron, pawing at it and whining. We could clearly hear a baby crying.

Ushering the dog away, we carefully removed the corrugated iron and other pieces of debris, wood, and some bricks until a hollow was revealed beneath a small sheet of plywood. Clicking on his flashlight, Charlie peered in.

"Sweet Jesus, there's a baby in there," he said.

Removing the last bits of detritus, Charlie reached in and drew out a small bundle wrapped in a pink and white woollen coverlet. Nat took the bundle from him and pulled back the edge of the blanket, revealing a pink-faced, blue-eyed baby looking up at her and cooing. Nat let the baby take her finger, murmuring softly to it. The baby stopped crying.

As if by magic, the dog stopped barking and flopped to the ground. Its sides heaving, he looked at each of us in turn but mostly at Nat and her precious charge. Its tongue lolled out the side of its mouth like a dry piece of white leather.

Then it hit me.

"You clever boy," I said, kneeling by the dog and ruffling the fur at its neck. He looked at me with shining eyes, tail beating a fierce tattoo

on the hard ground. "Good boy," I praised, "good boy."

"I don't get it," Charlie said, perplexed.

I grinned at him. "He wasn't barking *at* the Creep; he was barking *because* of the Creeps, to cover the baby's crying. For some reason, the Creeps ignore other animals, and somehow the dog knew that. It knew if the baby's cries were heard, the Creeps would come running."

"Jesus, you think?" said Charlie, amazed.

"The baby's not crying and the dog's quiet, speaks for itself," I said, still fussing the panting dog.

"How did the baby get here?" asked Andrew.

"Look around. Check the farmhouse and the barn. Maybe we'll find some clue as to what happened here."

I turned to Linda and Nat.

"Take the baby back to the van; get it out of this heat."

Linda nodded and led the way, and Nat followed with the baby. The dog padded alongside Nat, reluctant to relinquish his responsibility over its tiny charge.

A brief search gave up the parents about fifty yards away behind a crumbling wall. They must have hidden the baby and then tried to lead the Creeps away. The condition of their bodies left no doubt that Creeps were responsible for the horrific mutilation they had suffered. It cost them their lives, but the baby survived.

"Should we bury them?" asked Andrew, white-faced.

"We haven't the time," I said, "and staying here is too risky."

I could feel the woodlands pressing in on me. We were lingering too long, and the chances of the Creeps returning was too great.

"We'll put them together, side-by-side, and cover them with stones from the wall," I said.

Back at the van, Nat was sitting in the front, using a plastic teaspoon to feed the baby some milk from one of the thermos flasks. The dog lay in the shade of the van by the open passenger door, keeping a watchful eye.

"I don't know how long he's been barking like that," said Linda, "but he downed two bowls of water."

"He's a clever dog," I said, fussing the Collie once again. "He's going to be a welcome addition to our family." I looked at the baby in Nat's arms, its eyes dreamy with sleep, a contented smile on its cherubic face. "And so is she."

Sixteen

"What a precious little thing," Sally said, taking the baby in her arms. "What beautiful blue eyes, and that smile."

"She's an orphan," Nat said. "Creeps..."

"I'll check her over," Sally said, still fussing the baby, "but she looks none the worse for wear."

"She's one of the family now," Nat said, gently stroking the baby's face. "Our youngest member."

Sally took the baby into the coach. As Nat turned away, I saw an odd expression in her eyes.

"It's a shit world," she said thickly as she passed me.

"Nat?"

She stopped and looked at me. "It's up to us, Adam. We've got to give these kids a future, and we've got to give them back their lives."

"And we will, Nat, I promise," I said.

She nodded and walked off, her head down.

The dog whined anxiously as the baby disappeared into the coach. It was torn between its instinct to protect and the attention he was enjoying from the kids crowding around him, delighted with their new friend.

Now that I had the time, I realised the dog was larger than any Border Collie I'd ever seen. I thought back on the brutes I had encountered back at Denford Park. This Collie was bigger than normal, but it wasn't aggressive or vicious like those brutes. I briefly wondered if I should keep an eye on the dog to watch for any signs of aggression. Border Collies were renowned for their temperate natures, their intelligence and friendliness, except with other dogs. As was their nature, they were usually a one-man dog, working to herd sheep in the fields and hills of Wales and Scotland. Seeing the dog watching attentively over the baby, I didn't think there was anything to worry about.

The kid's administrations won out, and the Collie, obviously deciding the baby was in safe hands, barked joyously as he played happily with the children, racing around their legs with its bushy tail wagging furiously.

"We're going to have to give them both a name," said Linda beside me.

I slipped my arm around her waist and drew her close. "I thought the ladies could name the baby, and the kids the dog," I said. "Make it some sort of competition; best name wins a bar of chocolate or something."

"Becoming quite the domestic leader, aren't you?" Linda said, cocking an eyebrow at me.

"Just seems to grow on you," I said, giving a short laugh.

"You're a natural," she said, hugging me.

Being shaded under the walkway out of the blistering sun was a relief as the afternoon wore on. Tom Taylor and his team returned, having experienced as much luck as we had—food, bottled water, tools, and another van, a Mercedes High Cube, which Tom was driving. Another surprise was the 1,000cc BMW Touring motorcycle that Roger, Jeff, and Alan were unloading from the back of the Mercedes.

"I saw Pete this morning as we rode out," Roger said. "I saw his face. He's ready to ride again, and it is his bike."

"So you found your own," I said.

"Seemed the obvious solution," Roger said.

"Absolutely," I agreed.

"I picked up a full set of leathers, helmet, boots, the lot. I'm all set to go," said Roger. "Pete's denims were ruined, ripped and covered in blood. I guessed his size and got him some leathers too, if he wants them." As he spoke, Roger had a strange look in his eyes, not worry exactly but close.

I suddenly realised that Roger was worried that he wouldn't be needed as a scout any longer.

"Pete will appreciate the thought," I said, "and a third scout will be very handy. I'm pleased for you, Roger."

The look of relief on his face was touching.

"Cheers, Adam, that's great." He walked away a happy man.

Pete Hogan was over by his bike at the edge of the motorway, walking around it, crouching down, examining this and that. He stood up and shook his head.

"You sure you're up to riding that thing?" I asked.

"Try and stop me," Pete said, another happy man.

I've never had the same enthusiasm for motorbikes.

Pete walked around the gleaming machine again. "It's immaculate," he said. "We've been on the road, what, a week? There's not a mark on her, not a single speck of dust, and she's running as sweet as a nut."

"I'm not surprised," I said. "Roger loves engines; it was never in safer hands."

"I can see that," said Pete. "I thought I was particular." He lovingly ran his finger along the chrome handlebars.

"Well, it made Roger's day being able to ride scout. You won't need to thank him; riding your bike was thanks enough for him. Oh, and he's got something for you. You should go see him."

"It'll be good riding with him," Pete said, watching as Roger showed off his new toy to Nat and the Taylor boys. "And I'd like to express my appreciation…"

I wasn't happy about camping under the motorway's walkway for another night. Having the woods so close made me nervous. There were people on watch, armed but keeping a low profile, keeping their weapons out of sight, so it wouldn't alarm the children. I had quietly told some of the others to keep alert and have their weapons close but discreet. As a final precaution, Linda and I wandered about the small camp, being sociable but surreptitiously keeping an eye on our surroundings. Dark shadows loomed on either side of the road, pressing in on the meagre lights of the

arc lamps and torches. The oil drum fire was a mere glow in the darkness.

The baby was causing quite a stir. The children crowded around Sally where she bounced the toddler on her knee, much to the baby's delight. Her tinkling laugh was infectious. After a very brief discussion amongst themselves, the women and children came up with a name—a very appropriate name as it turned out. She was the first baby we had seen up close for over a year, and the first baby brought into our family. Eve.

The dog still didn't have a name, but it seemed happy enough with everyone just calling him "Boy." Tricia was planning a naming competition in the morning. She had already told the children to put their thinking caps on overnight and think of as many names as they could. The children were only too eager to comply.

"Still no change in Tina?" Linda asked.

We were standing at the edge of the camp by the cab. As usual, the night was warm and very black. We were in a strange, near-empty world where life as we knew it was struggling for survival; a nightmare world where nature, once my truest friend, had become the enemy. I listened for the sounds of the night but could hear none, just the soft whisper of the unseen trees in the darkness as the wind soughed through their branches. I seemed to have little time to myself these days—a state alien to my nature. Eighteen months ago, I had been in Scotland near Applecross Pass, a twelve-mile road that led up over the mountains into Applecross Village.

I had planned to return there in November to test my skills in a winter camp, then this shit hit. Now, I was going back to Scotland for completely different reasons. I held Linda tighter in my arms, holding her close. Moments like this with her had become precious and as rare as hen's teeth. And now, we had acquired a gooseberry. The Border Collie sat on its haunches beside us, quietly looking into the night.

"None," I said in answer to Linda's question. "She's eating and taking better care of herself, though Sally still helps her. She won't talk and rarely gets out of bed except to go to the bathroom."

"When we get to Scotland, it will be different," Linda said. "We'll be settled, more stable. Tina will come out of herself then."

"I hope so," I said. "I want her to be as she was when I first met her; you would have liked her. She was easy to get along with. The twins are fretting for her too. They're wondering what's happened to their mum; they don't understand. She does talk to them, thankfully, but it's like Tina thinks they are two years old, y'know? Talking to them like babies."

"It gives her comfort," Linda said. "Maybe reliving better times rather than the horror she went through."

"I guess," I said dubiously.

"Adam, when we get to Scotland, we will build a whole new community. Maybe we'll find an abandoned village with ready-made homes just in need of a little TLC and restoration or maybe a large farm with lots of outbuildings that we can make secure and turn into liveable cottages. Our options are endless. Look at what

we've got working for us: electricians, builders, mechanics..." She smiled up at me. "Hunters."

I hugged her, kissing the top of her head. "Don't ever stop kicking me up the arse," I said.

"You don't ever stop needing me to," she said and kissed me.

The Collie whined at our feet as if to say, "Get a room for God's Sake!"

Checking the map, I realised what I had mistaken for a small wood was in fact the beginnings of Sherwood Forest, a vast expanse of trees which spread over a thousand acres, mainly pine with areas of oak, birch, chestnut, and beech. It was home to the famous Major Oak, purportedly the oldest oak in England, estimated to be between 800-1,000 years old. I visited it once—the fabled home of Robin Hood and his Merry Men—and was disappointed to find the old oak's massive branches had to be supported by wooden beams. Although, if I was a thousand years old, I guess I would need supporting too. It was still majestic in its infirmity, making it easy to imagine how the legend of Robin Hood had arisen in the huge greenwood.

I felt a twinge of sadness at the thought that I might never walk beneath those ancient trees again.

I was anxious to move on, but finding the twin goldmines in Derby and Nottingham made that impossible; we had to plunder both to capacity.

"Maybe Tom had the right idea: maybe we should get more vans," said Charlie.

"I was thinking the same," said Andrew.

"It not about more vans," I said. "They're easy to get. It's the logistics that's the problem. The more vehicles we have, the more fuel we will need. Very soon, it's going to be a scarce commodity. Motor vehicles will become obsolete unless there's a massive reversal of fortune in the world's future. We need to find a large source of fuel, but in the meantime, we need to ration what we have."

"Maybe we can find a tanker; there's bound to be at least one on our way to Scotland," Terry put in. "If we can get it to Scotland, it could set us up for years if we're careful."

"Let's not get too far ahead of ourselves," I said. "I appreciate your enthusiasm, but we need to travel light and fast. We have plenty of supplies now; there's nothing else we need.

"Our best bet is to get to Scotland, establish ourselves, and get a community up and running. Once we are secured, then we can start scavenging the surrounding areas and check out the cities: Inverness, Edinburgh, Glasgow.

"If my guess is right, we are liable to find other people there, and we won't know their disposition, so we'll have to tread carefully. On the brighter side, I think we'll be safe from both the vines and Creeps, but that's still not an absolute."

"What sort of time frame are we talking to get to Scotland?" asked Sean.

"Originally, we intended to take it slow and easy once we were clear of London, a joint decision, but I think we should rethink that," I said.

"Rethink it?" queried Charlie.

"I was going to suggest we move a little faster to make better time," I said.

"I thought the idea was to take it slowly, see what's in front of us," Julie said.

"It still is," I agreed, "but like I said, we have everything we need. The road between here and Scotland is much the same as we've experienced so far. In normal circumstances we could get to Scotland in twelve, maybe eighteen, hours. We still don't have to rush, but I think we should push though and get there within one, maybe two days, no more malingering."

"Why this change of mind?" asked Roger.

"I was thinking mainly of the children and Tina," I said. "Extended travelling, living on a coach, stopping at potentially hostile campsites. I want to give them the security that they deserve, that they need. It's difficult while we're on the road."

"I see what you're saying," said Trish. "And you're right, they need a home and the stability that comes with it, but at the moment, they're fine, especially with the dog. It's just one big adventure to them."

"All the same, I think we should push on. Things are only going to get harder out here, and I don't want a repeat of Newport. Next time, we might not be so lucky."

"You think there are more gangs like that?" Julie asked.

"Without scaremongering, I think it's inevitable," I said frankly. "The longer we're on the road, the more likely."

I could feel them stirring uncomfortably at the thought.

"Then let's get moving," said Sally. "Get to Scotland as quick as we can."

"We don't have to go right now, Sal." I laughed. "We can give the children their morning. Trish and Joan have something planned for the kids.

We'll go salvage the rest of the supplies while that's going on and make a start early afternoon."

A strange thing happened the following morning. I intended to go with Charlie and the others to get the supplies, but the Border Collie refused to stay behind. He literally dogged my every step, wanting to go with me.

"Hey boy," I ruffled his neck, "the kids need you here. They're giving you a name later."

The children clamoured around, calling out several names, but the dog didn't respond to any of them. He just sat in front of me, tail thrashing the air, tongue lolling.

"What's the matter with him?" asked Charlie.

"I think he sees Adam as his new master," Linda said.

"Why's he picked me?" I laughed. "He's supposed to belong to everyone."

"I don't think anyone's told him that," said Charlie.

I tried to shoo the dog away, but he wasn't having it.

"Look at that," said Charlie with a grin. "One word from you, and he does exactly as he pleases."

"Very funny," I said. "You've got to stay here, boy," I said, looking at the dog.

His tail continued to wag furiously.

"You'll have to stay here," said Linda, "or you'll disappoint the kids. If you stay, he'll stay."

"But the supplies...?" I protested.

"We can handle them, dog whisperer..." Charlie said.

Trish and Joan had outdone themselves. Days ago, they had given Alan and Jeff a list of things originally intended for a birthday party for one of the children. A portable gazebo had been erected and two tables were laid out with various sweets, biscuits, and, amazingly, two cakes which Sally had baked on a barbeque. I didn't even begin to ask how even though I knew how to make bread with the aid of a Dutch oven. There were party hats and decorations all over the gazebo. Bunting fluttered in the wind—bright red, blue, green, and yellow—complimented by colourful balloons fixed firmly in place. Lemonade and orange juice flowed.

Watching from the side-lines as various games were played, the dog at my feet, I laughed along with the kids as they squealed with delight, playing pass the parcel, musical chairs, and pin the tail on the donkey. Nursery rhymes blasted from a battery powered CD player. They sang "Happy Birthday" to Bobby Gray who was ten years old, eagerly tearing open the presents he had received: action figures, a football, and a remote-controlled truck.

On a smaller table, brightly decorated with crepe paper and ribbons, sat a blue box with a tight-fitting lid. I didn't need to look inside to know it was filled with scraps of paper, neatly folded to hide what was written on them.

Hearing the children's gleeful laughter would have melted a miser's heart as they enjoyed their celebration. It didn't matter a whit that the world might be dying or that they had been torn from their homes and families. Right now, they were happy and having a good time. I was pleased to see Tina, wrapped up in a light blanket, sitting in a camp chair by the door of the coach, a timorous smile playing on her pale lips. Sally was standing beside her, a comforting hand resting on Tina's shoulder. I went and stood with them, the dog trotting along behind me.

Sally smiled at me; little Eve was nestled in the crook of her arm cooing quietly to herself. I smiled back, looking briefly down at Tina who didn't even acknowledge my presence. Sally gave a small shrug of her shoulders as our eyes met, unified in our silent grief at the loss of our friend's happiness.

The day was getting hot; the kids were sweating profusely, their gleaming faces happy and red.

"Okay, okay!" Tricia clapped her hands for attention. "I think it's time for the big moment."

The children squealed and danced with excitement, gathering around Trish, jostling and pushing for pride of place.

"It's time for the big draw." Tricia continued to play to the children's anticipation. "There are several big prizes for the winner: chocolate, a can of Coca Cola, and a large packet of chewy sweets," Tricia said as Joan brought over the blue box. "Let's see who has thought of the best name for the newest member of our family."

Taking the box Trish shook it, the paper inside rustling loudly. "I've given them a good shake up," she teased, "but who's going to make the draw?"

Of course, everyone's hand shot up with cries of "me, me, me!"

I had to laugh, as did Sally and some of the remaining adults. I was pleased to see a hesitant smile lighten Tina's face.

"Well, I think we need someone who hasn't voted," said Tricia, "so there's no cheating."

The children were getting frantic.

"Adam!" she called. "Would you do the honours?"

Cheers erupted; the children began chanting my name.

"Me?" I said in mock reticence. The chanting got louder. "How can I refuse?" I said, laughing.

I put my hand into the box and rummaged around, taking my time. The kids fell silent, watching with expectant eyes. I drew out the piece of paper and handed it to Tricia. You could have heard a pin drop.

"Well..." Tricia said, opening the piece of paper. "What a wonderful name!"

"Tell us! Tell us!" the children whooped.

Smiling broadly, Tricia said, "And the winner is..." she paused to add drama, "Tag, suggested by Susie Yarrow!"

Susie Yarrow screamed excitedly, her friends holding her and clapping her on the back as they all jumped up and down.

Tricia called the dog to her, crouching down and putting her arms around his shaggy neck.

"Let me introduce Tag, the family dog!" she announced. "And because everybody made such a good effort thinking up all those wonderful names, I think everybody should have a prize!"

The cheers and squeals were deafening.

Seventeen

I was happy. As crazy as that sounds in a world that was going to shit, but I was happy. We had picked up the A1 just north of Leeds and were making good time. I was reminded of an old song, "Convoy" by C.W. McCall, especially when I saw Sean's Kombi tucked in behind the coach, rolling along in front of Jeff's van, I couldn't remember the words exactly, something about "Long-haired" and "Jesus."

Since we left Sherwood Forest behind us, there was little green to be seen over the last stretch of motorway. There was still evidence of extensive burning—whether by design or another fire out of control, there was no way to tell. There wasn't any significant drop in temperature as we progressed farther north. I expected the weather to change some, but the sun was still blazing in a clear blue sky as the road lay empty before us. I was a little worried.

Mike Oldfield was playing on my MP3 player as we cruised at a steady sixty-five. Linda and Roger were up front, and Pete brought up the rear. Our exit was about an hour away, and it wouldn't be much longer before we crossed over into Scotland. The prospect relaxed me; all concerns and worries were just falling away.

Normally, I wouldn't have come this far up the A1, but I wanted to bypass the Lake District. It was a wrench to my heart as the lakes had always been a favourite place for me, but now I figured it was a vine-infested death trap. It was just speculation on my part, but I wasn't prepared to find out the truth the hard way.

I had many fond memories of my times in the Lake District, hiking across the length and breadth of the mountains and fells, the valleys and the hills, swimming and kayaking on the lakes. I was already imagining Windemere and Buttermere choked with vines and Creeps running rampant through the picturesque villages: Grasmere, Coniston, Ambleside. I pushed the thoughts away, not wanting to darken the day with unnecessary gloom.

Linda and Roger planned to wait at Scotch Corner, the exit to the A66 which would take us across country to Penrith and the M6 North. It was a more direct route that would bring us into Glasgow where we would begin the last leg of our journey into the Western Highlands. We would still touch on the Lake District National Park at Penrith, though I didn't anticipate any problems; we would trundle right past the danger area without stopping. As we rolled north, I became more and more convinced that this crazy scheme could actually work.

Linda was stretched out on her bike, using her helmet as a pillow and enjoying the sun as the convoy reached the meeting place. She raised an eyebrow at me as I got out of the cab.

"Took your time." She grinned.

I leaned down and kissed her. "No need to get up," I said.

She laughed and swung her legs round. "There's a good place to camp on the south side of the roundabout. Looks like a truck stop. We cruised it but didn't go inside. That..." she said, indicating a large red bricked building behind us, "is a police station. What's weird is that it's also a Holiday Inn, very strange. But it might be worth checking out, maybe a more comfortable place to spend the night. And down there is the A66 to Penrith."

"Good job," I said surveying the area. "There's been a lot of burning here."

"I'd say that was down to the close proximity of the police station," Roger said as he came to join us. He looked good in his new black leathers and gleaming ice blue crash helmet. "They would have acted at the first sign of trouble."

"Probably right," I said. "The area here is pretty open. Do you think it's worth driving to the truck stop?"

Linda shrugged. "I can't imagine there's anything there we might need. Maybe Alan and Jeff can check it out. You want to stay here?"

"Why not?" I nodded at the police station. "Ready-made security and maybe we can use the hotel rooms."

"I'll check them out," said Linda.

"No, I'll get Charlie and Sean," I said. "You can carry on relaxing."

"Yeah, right," she said.

I should have known better.

The doors to the police station were half open—two heavy wooden affairs made from oak or maybe mahogany. Beyond were two more modern glass doors giving way to a large reception area.

"The air's a bit stale in here," Sean said through the gloom.

"Long time empty," said Charlie, his torch beam highlighting the disturbed dust motes in the airless room.

It felt musty and cloying; all the windows were boarded up, and it was hard to breathe.

"The offices are over there," I said. "It looks as if the holding cells are downstairs."

"Doubt if anyone's home." Charlie grinned, the backlight from his torch highlighting his strong white teeth and the sardonic gleam in his eyes.

"Sean," I said, ignoring Charlie's pun, "you check the office. Charlie, you poke around in here. I'll check out downstairs."

No light permeated the stairs, so I clicked on my flashlight as I descended. The air was thicker down here; it felt claustrophobic. The wooden door at the bottom was unlocked. Beyond was a short corridor with a heavily secured door at the farther end—a fire exit. Three steel doors painted a dull flat grey colour were on each side of the corridor and six cells, each with a sliding observation panel, situated in its centre.

My trainers squeaked on the vinyl floor as I went to the first cell; it was locked. *Why would it be locked?* I wondered, frowning. A tingle touched the back of my neck as I tentatively unbolted the observation panel and slid it back.

The smell wasn't strong, but it was sharp, acrid, as I shone my torch into the cell.

"Oh shit…" Recoiling from the door, I gagged, the sight within seared into my retinas.

Body bags, lots of them, some ballooned from the malodorous gasses escaping from the decaying bodies stacked high within the cell. Too late, I slammed shut the panel, breathing heavily.

"Shit, shit, shit," I gasped, leaning down, my hands on my knees, trying to suck in what air there was in the dark, oppressive corridor

Reluctantly, I checked the other cells. All contained dead, decaying bodies, but not all of them were in body bags; some were wrapped up in plastic sheeting or tarpaulins.

"Adam! Up here!" Sean's deep voice resonated through the building.

I took the stairs two at a time, my haste not solely due to the urgency in Sean's voice. He was waiting for me in the reception area, his normally ruddy face pale and sweating.

"In there," he indicated.

Charlie stood by the front doors, equally pale.

I briefly looked into the back office, already knowing what I was going to see. More body bags and the added extra of two uniformed policemen, their cadaverous skin as brown as parchment, the cheeks sunken, the eyes gone. I shut the door.

"It seems they didn't realise the danger of the vines until it was too late," said Sean.

There was no answer to that.

"Let's get out of here," I said thickly.

"Any good?" Linda asked as we exited the building.

Sean pulled the main doors closed after we exited, forcing a length of timber through the door handles so no one else's curiosity would get the better of them.

"We'll camp at the truck stop," I said tightly.

Linda looked puzzled, especially when she saw the haunted look on Sean and Charlie's faces.

"Adam?"

"Don't ask," I said.

We left early the next morning. I was more determined than ever to press on to Scotland.

"Oh my God..." Linda's voice was as soft as a feather settling on silk when I told her about our discovery in the police station.

"There must have been at least a hundred bodies, maybe more," I said. "Wrapped in anything waterproof that they could find."

"Who were they?" she asked as we lay together in a quiet corner of the transport café. We had portioned off a makeshift room by stretching a blanket between two pillars; a light sleeping bag was draped over us, though we didn't really need it.

"Townspeople, I guess. Casualties of the vines or black Dust or maybe Creeps. There was no way to tell. I wasn't about to look any closer."

"The survivors must have been evacuated," said Linda. "God knows where..."

"Had to better than here," I said. "I think they torched everything in sight, probably hoping it would take the police station with it."

"Those poor people..." Linda said sorrowfully.
"Yeah..." I said, staring into the darkness.

Morning brought another bright, sunny day.
I let the convoy go on ahead. Sean and Linda
stayed behind with me. Once the coach was out
of sight, we doused the police station in liberal
amounts of petrol, concentrating on the base-
ment. We couldn't afford to waste the fuel, but
I couldn't stand the thought of all those rotting corpses lying there; it was undignified
somehow, and they deserved better. Also, I
didn't relish the thought of some unsuspecting
traveller stumbling on the sights within. I
wouldn't wish that on anyone. I threw the
burning petrol-soaked rag into the building's
foyer. There was a *whump* as the fire took hold,
turning the interior of the building scarlet with
dancing light. Sean and I drove away in the cab,
Linda following on her bike. This time we had
made sure the flames did their job.

Eighteen

We made Penrith in good time but didn't stop, moving straight on and bypassing Carlisle before finally stopping at a small services, Todhills. I pulled in preceding the coach and smiled as I saw Linda and Roger checking all around the place, taking special notice of the exits. *Once bitten...*

We stayed the night with no incidents and left two hours after sunrise. We were about twenty miles from Gretna Green and eighteen from the English-Scottish border, marked by the River Sark. It was as we were approaching Gretna that I first started seeing signs of a possible problem. Abandoned cars, scattered haphazardly across the road, were becoming more prolific, forcing Charlie to swerve in and out. I could see he was having more and more difficulty getting through.

"Charlie, pull over," I said. "Let's check what's ahead."

"I was about to suggest that very thing," he returned back. "It's like being in the Dodgem's at the fun fair, only it's not so much fun."

"It's blocked, Adam, totally," Linda said over the radio.

"Shit…" I swore, then keyed the mike. "No way round?"

"No, we'll have to go back, get off the motorway, and find another road."

"If we go back to Junction 44 we can pick up the A7 to Langholm, then cut east along the 'B' road to the A74, and then turn north," Charlie said, tracing his finger over the map.

"The whole area is heavily forested," I said. "I don't know if they're safe or not."

"What's the difference?" asked Linda. "Sooner or later, we are going to have to find out."

"I guess," I said, thoughtfully rubbing the stubble on my chin.

The route Charlie had laid out was our best option. I couldn't see any other road on the map that didn't cut through a wood or forest.

"Okay, but we tighten up our formation. You and Roger keep close; no going off on your own."

Linda looked at me askance.

"I mean it, Lin. Just until we clear the woodlands."

It was a bit of a mission to turn the coach around, but we were soon on our way again. The A7 was a long, narrow road without room to manoeuvre, and I hoped that nothing blocked the way ahead. Perhaps I was getting paranoid, but I didn't like the proximity of the limited road after the wide-open freedom of the motorway. Seeing Linda and Roger stop on the crest of a small rise ahead didn't alleviate my concern one iota.

"Look," Linda said as I reached them.

The white Escort van was in a ditch, tilted at a crazy angle, its back doors flung wide.

"It's Chris' and Harmony's van," said Roger.

"Damn," I said.

He was right. I recognised the distinctive bright coloured Sunflower motif on the back door. A quick call from Linda halted the convoy while Roger and I cautiously approached the clearly abandoned van. While they kept watch, I looked inside.

I'm not sure what I expected to find—blood or dead bodies. After Scotch Corner, I didn't think anything else could freak me out again, even though my mouth had suddenly gone dry. Thankfully, there was neither, nor were there any keys in the ignition. The floor in the rear was ripped up, revealing a hidden compartment beneath. Linda rummaged through the wreckage. "Adam." She held up a small cellophane packet. "It says 'Abstract Morphine.'"

"Bastards did steal it," I growled.

"There's a mattress dumped in the ditch here and clothes, designer," said Roger.

"Seems they left in a hurry," I said.

"Or they were taken," Linda said ominously.

A hurried search of the immediate area revealed nothing. Judging by his expression, Roger was relieved there were no bodies too. Truth be told, so was I.

"There's nothing for us here," I said

I felt the tension that the scene generated. The van, the drugs, the disappearance of Chris and Harmony—it definitely didn't feel right. I told Charlie to come ahead but to put his foot down. The motorway was only a couple of

miles ahead, and the quicker we were off the "A" road, the better.

Was it good judgement or just dumb luck? I'll never know. The motorway was less than a mile away when a small flatbed truck roared out from behind a large pile of dirt on the right-hand side of the road, directly in front of the speeding coach. Charlie hauled on the wheel, and the coach lurched to the right, clipping the rear of the truck and spinning it away like a kid's toy. It barely slowed the bus down.

"Charlie! Go! Go!" I yelled into the radio.

Linda and Roger had already passed and were in the clear. I took position behind the coach, and the rest of the convoy followed. A second truck, bigger than the first, pulled out onto the road. Whoever they were, they missed the coach but cut off the rest of us. A third lorry appeared—a dumper truck. I braked and pulled to the side of the road.

Using the cab as cover, I watched as the others pulled over. Sean and Tom Taylor took up position behind the Kombi. Thankfully, Brendan, Sean's son, had opted to ride in the coach with the other kids for company.

We were surrounded by open fields; our only cover was our own vehicles.

"Just walk away! Leave the vehicles and walk away and no one gets hurt!" The voice was grating, harsh.

"Not going to happen!" I called back. "You need to back off. Let us pass."

Automatic gun fire resounded, splitting the still air.

"Does it sound as if I need to back off? We're not fucking around, man. Go now, while you can."

"There's only a couple of them, Adam; we can take them," said Tom.

"We don't know for certain," I returned. "Keep under cover; let me handle this."

"We should flank him, use the ditch as cover," Alan added.

"No, stay down," I commanded.

"Give it up, man, walk away!" yelled the thug.

"Listen to me, we don't want any trouble..."

"Then walk away," the gunman yelled back.

"You know we can't do that."

"It's not a suggestion..."

They had chosen their ambush site well; there were wide drainage ditches either side of the road and high mounds of earth for cover. I figured they had some sort of makeshift bridge over the ditch to allow egress over the trench and open fields all around. The only way was forward—or back.

The sound of another engine roared behind us, but our vehicles prevented me seeing what was happening. Tyres screeched and a short burst of gunfire split the still air.

What the hell? I keyed my radio, "What's happening back there?"

"No problem, Adam," Pete Hogan returned grimly. "Some guy thought he'd block the road behind us; I convinced him otherwise."

"Okay, watch our back door in case we have to make a break for it. Don't do anything stupid."

"Will do."

The gunfire caught the thug's attention, and he craned his neck to see past our vehicles, his expression somewhat disconcerted.

"Just pull your trucks off the road, and we'll be on our way," I yelled, swiping the stinging sweat from my face with my bandaged forearm.

"You Adam?"

What the fuck? How does everyone we meet know my name? Hearing my name was a shock.

"Who are you?" I yelled, trying to keep my voice level.

"We got mutual friends..."

Sean and Tom were easing their way forward to a better position. Nat was working her way toward me, using the vans as cover.

"How the hell does he know your name?" Jeff asked.

"No idea. I was just wondering the same," I replied.

The sound of a scuffle brought my attention back to the thug. Another man was dragging two people out from behind the flatbed. He forced them to their knees in the middle of the road. It was Chris Scott and Harmony Quaid, looking the worse for wear.

"Mystery solved," said Jeff wryly.

"A little more incentive," the thug called, pointing the gun at Chris' head.

"Now what?" asked Sean.

"These two say they know you, say you got a ton of food and supplies. We can trade..."

Both thugs were twitchy, constantly swiping at their noses with their shirt cuffs. It wasn't the heat that sheened their faces with sweat.

Fuck, I thought.

"You got two minutes to decide," the thug yelled.

"We've got to do something," Alan said anxiously. "I know Chris and Harmony are arseholes, but we can't just leave them to the mercy of that maniac."

"It's worse than that," I said. "I think they're high."

"What?" Sean asked.

"I think they have availed themselves of the drugs provided by Chris."

"Wonderful," Tom said dryly.

"Okay, let's try not to spook them," I said. "Tom, you and Andrew make your way along the right-hand ditch…"

Nat appeared beside me, her face grim.

"Nat, Terry, take the left-hand ditch…"

"I'm with Terry," came a voice.

"Teresa, what the hell? You're supposed to be on the coach."

"I'm with Terry," she simply repeated.

Nat looked at me and shrugged.

"Okay, go with Terry, but keep low and be careful."

"Me, Jeff, and Alan have the middle covered," said Sean.

Nat was watching the thugs through the cab's windows.

"There's at least three of them," she said, "and I think you're right, they're as high as kites, which makes them unpredictable."

"Maybe we can use that against them," I said.

"There's six of them," came a voice from the radio.

"Charlie! What are you doing here? Where's the coach?" I said in amazement.

"Julie's taken it out onto the motorway; I figured you might need some help. I got Paul and Stephen with me, so is Roger and Linda."

"Okay," I said, shaking my head in exasperation. "No one move till I give the word." I turned to Nat. "It just gets worse."

"It's what families do," she said pointedly.

"Keep an eye on those two thugs," I said.

Opening the boot of the cab, I pulled out a rifle case. I hadn't used the AGM air rifle in weeks, but I had a use for it now. I knelt by the rear of the cab, sighting the scope.

"What are you going to do?" asked Nat.

"At this range the slug won't kill him, but it will bloody hurt. We need to distract them long enough to get past," I explained.

"But their van's in the way," she said.

"It won't be when you ram it with the cab." I grinned. "Hit it from the rear, push it into the ditch."

She looked at me dubiously.

"I'm betting the driver is sitting with the truck in gear, his foot on the clutch," I said.

"If you say so," Nat returned, "but the cab will be wrecked."

"I'll buy a new one," I said and winked.

"Okay, listen up," I said into the radio, "this is what we're going to do..."

Nineteen

"Enough fucking about!" yelled the thug before jamming the muzzle of the gun against Chris' head. "Move out! Now!"

Settling myself, I took aim, sighting on the gunman's head. I'd told Nat the slug wouldn't be lethal at this range; I hoped I was right. It was a tense moment. I calmed my breathing, sighted, and squeezed the trigger.

Screaming, the man fell back, dropping his gun as he clutched at his face. I saw bright red trickle through his fingers as he dropped to the ground. Immediately, Sean, Terry, and Teresa opened fire, the fusillade aimed high, designed to frighten and confuse rather than injure anyone. The panels at the rear of the van made a hell of a din as bullets smacked into sheet metal.

The second thug dragged his mate to cover as Nat fired up the cab and accelerated toward the obstructing van. I retreated back into the ditch as gunfire was returned. It was erratic and confusing; they were firing blindly in our general direction. As haphazard as it was, it was nonetheless dangerous.

Using my Glock, I joined the withering barrage, aiming for metal to gain the loudest effect.

I winced as I heard the cab smash into the rear of the truck, tyres screaming as they fought to gain purchase and force the truck into the ditch.

I switched aim and fired a few hasty shots through the truck's windscreen. It exploded into the cab, showering the inside with sparkling glass. The truck shot forward, aided by the taxi. I was right—the driver had been riding the clutch. Other engines roared into life as our vans rolled forward, hauling the trailers behind them. Nat, Terry, and Teresa scrambled to board the Mercedes.

Linda and Roger roared into the fray, skidding to a stop in front of the kneeling couple. They leapt off their motorbikes, and knives flashed in the sun as Linda cut Harmony's bonds and hauled her onto the bike's pillion. Astride the machine, Linda roared off as Roger struggled with Chris.

One of the vans stopped to allow Charlie, Tom, and Andrew aboard before quickly pulling away. Closely followed by the Mercedes, the vans tore through the gap and away. Maureen McCormick brought up the Kombi; only Sean and I were left. Bullets still flew as Sean crouched by the VW, laying down sporadic covering fire as I scrambled from the ditch, firing as I came.

Roger was having problems with Chris who seemed dazed and disoriented. Roger could barely hold the staggering man as he helped him onto the bike. As I crossed the open ground, I watched anxiously as Chris struggled to mount the bike. Firing in the general direction of the cowering thugs, I was relieved to see Roger get on the bike and pull away.

The gunman appeared by the truck that Nat had shoved into the ditch. He held the automatic rifle low in his hand and opened fire; the gun barked its lethal chatter toward the fleeing motorbike. Roger swerved as red flowers bloomed on the back of Chris's white shirt, stitching a line left to right. The bike wobbled as Chris slumped, veered, and crashed onto its side in a shower of sparks, hurling the two men across the tarmac.

"Roger!" I fired several shots at the gunman as he ducked behind the shelter of his van.

Chris lay face down on the roadway, unmoving. I saw Roger stagger to his feet, shaking his helmeted head. He barely took two steps toward Chris when strong hands grabbed me by the shoulders and hurled me into the Kombi through the side door.

"Go! Go! Go!" Sean yelled at his wife.

"Stop by Roger!" I yelled, scrambling to my knees to look out of the windscreen. Bullets kerranged into the Kombi's bodywork; it was like being inside a kettle drum.

Roger swayed unsteadily on wide braced legs, shucking his helmet. Shaking his head, he gazed about, saw Chris, and stepped toward him when the machine gun clattered again. Roger spun away, arms flailing, and hit the ground hard.

"No!" I screamed, hauling the side door open.

I couldn't see the gunman, and I didn't care. Maureen stopped. As I stepped down from the van, bullets ricocheted at my feet, punching into the side door; chips of concrete whizzed through the air.

"It's no good! They'll get you too!" yelled Sean.

More bullets sprayed the side of the Kombi as Sean pulled me back in and slammed the door shut. The last thing I saw through the side window was Roger's face, his dead empty eyes staring up into a clear blue sky as we roared past.

"I could have got him!" I said angrily.

"No, you couldn't," Sean said quietly but firmly. "You would have gotten yourself killed and maybe me and Maureen with you."

"But ... we left him," I said dully, the anger beginning to drain out of me.

I slumped down onto the guardrail lining the motorway. I had never felt so tired. Two friends, good friends, family, were both lost within a week of each other. It was a terrible blow. First Jules and now Roger, probably the best among us—both needless, pointless deaths.

"We knew this might happen," Linda said softly, her hand on my shoulder.

"Doesn't make it any easier," I said. "Jesus! What the fuck's the matter with these people?"

"Can't we go back for them?" asked Terry.

"No. More than likely, they'll have reinforcements by now. We won't catch them by surprise a second time," Charlie said.

"What if we wait till tonight? It'll be dark in an hour or so," Julie suggested.

"It's too risky. They're alert now, and who knows what condition they'll be in; they were already high. They'll shoot first and ask questions after," Sean said.

"I don't like the thought of Roger just lying out there in the road," Sally said, her face creased.

"What if we offer a trade? Food for Roger and Chris," Teresa said.

"It's all or nothing for those bastards," Charlie said. "They won't bargain if they think we are weak."

"This is your fault!" Terry said, suddenly angry.

Harmony cowered on the steps of the coach, hugging herself, her face pale, and her lips a thin line. She was dirty, dishevelled, and her eyes haunted.

"I'm sorry," her voice was barely audible.

"Sorry?" Terry snapped. "What good's sorry? Roger's dead, left in the road like a stray dog and you're sorry? What the hell were you thinking? Why did you steal the bloody drugs in the first place?"

Flinching under the verbal barrage, Harmony swiped the tears from her face. "It was Chris's idea. He said we could use them for trade."

"Trade? With who? The world's gone to hell in a hand basket, and you still want to trade poison? What the fuck is the matter with you?"

I had never seen Terry so incensed. His dark eyes flashed angrily as he towered over the cringing Harmony.

"Tell us what happened?" Sally said, anxious to ease the mounting tension.

"Chris said supplies would become scarce, that we would starve unless we had something to trade. We found lots of stuff: jewellery, money, designer clothes, but it was all worthless. People wanted food, water, medical supplies. When he found the drugs in the medical tent back at the camp, he didn't think; he just took them."

"He robbed the people who were helping him?" Julie asked, her words tinged with disgust.

"Chris said it was turning into a dog-eat-dog world..."

"And you believed that, even though you were helped at the camp, and we brought you into our family?" Sally asked.

Harmony looked down at her hands and fiddled them in her lap.

"What else did you have hidden in your van?" asked Linda. "Is there anything else we need worry about?"

"Nothing," Harmony replied. "Designer clothes, perfume, make-up..."

"Jesus..." Charlie said, turning away.

"That's why you ran when the army turned up?" Nat asked.

"Chris panicked. I told him there was nothing to worry about, but he wouldn't listen."

"So why didn't you come back when the army left?" asked Charlie.

"Because we thought you had guessed what we'd done and turn us over to the army," she said dully. "We were going to drive to Scotland, get to Glasgow, and see if there were survivors there. Chris said there was sure to be or why else would you all be going to Scotland."

"To start our own community, to become self-sufficient," Alan said. "Why do you think we collected all these stores?"

"Chris said you were going to trade as well."

"Chris is, *was*, an arse," Charlie spat. "And it got him killed and took one of our friends with him, not to mention putting us and our children in danger."

Harmony sobbed into her hands.

"We should leave her here; she's nothing but trouble," Terry said darkly.

"No one gets left, whatever they've done," I said tiredly, looking hard at Terry. "You should think about that."

Terry returned my look. Rage still blazed in his eyes, but he said nothing more.

We were twenty miles from the ambush site, out of sight of the road in an industrial estate. I didn't think our attackers would follow us; they were probably too high or too disoriented by the brief unexpected resistance to bother us any further, but I wasn't taking any chances. As Julie said, we had a couple of hours of daylight left, and I wanted to put as much distance between us and them as possible.

The confrontation and the loss of Roger had demoralised us. I blamed myself. I had let my guard down and become careless. I think the actuality of our ongoing situation was finally coming home to some of the others. Suddenly, it wasn't so much as a jolly day trip in the country or a happy holiday. The real danger was apparent, and it had shaken them.

"Hilda..." Harmony said quietly. "Hilda Quinlen." She looked up miserably at the ring of faces surrounding her. "That's my real name."

No one said anything.

"Adam," Linda touched my shoulder, "we need to keep moving."

The day had taken its toll. There wasn't a smile to be seen. Everyone had the same haunted, defeated look in their eyes and bowed shoulders as if a crushing weight was pressing down on them. Even the children were quiet and subdued. I loved Roger like a brother. He had been quiet, unassuming, and he had always given his all, especially in his final act of bravery. Like Jules, I would have to mourn him later; the heaviness tearing at my insides would have to be put aside. Unlike Jules, Roger would not have the send-off he so richly deserved. That black thought made my heart even heavier.

Wearily, I got to my feet.

"We keep going for another hour, make sure we're not followed," I said. "We'll find somewhere to camp tonight and push on for Scotland tomorrow, and we don't stop until we get there."

"What about me?" Harmony—now Hilda—asked timorously.

"You go with Trish and Joan, help with the children. You are still a part of this family, but you've got a lot to prove," I said. "And until you do prove yourself, be warned: we are tolerant and won't just abandon you, but one more fuck up and I'll leave you at the next town. You will be fully provisioned and armed, but you'll be on your own. Do you understand?"

She nodded, relief all over her face. "I won't let you down," she said, her voice still trembled.

"Some of them aren't happy," Linda said when we were on our own.

"That's tough," I said. "We need to tighten up, Linda, stop playing games. They need to understand that this isn't going to be easy. They need to come to terms with that or none of us will survive. Abandoning people to the wild is never going to happen, not without giving them a chance to work with us, to be part of the family."

"I get that, but Terry doesn't and neither does Tom Taylor or his boys. They were close to Roger."

"Terry should know better," I said. "Tom and his boys will just have to deal with it too. Either they accept my leadership or what's the point? There's no time for this crap. We work together, or we don't work at all."

"Hey, calm down," Linda soothed. "We're fine, just shaken up, that's all; everybody's in shock."

My shoulders sagged. "I'm sorry. It's just that Roger..."

"Roger knew what he was doing. He knew the risks, and he was happy doing it; don't take that away from him."

I looked bleakly at her.

"Arse-kicker!" I said and found refuge in her arms, holding her close for long minutes.

"Adam! Come quick! Adam!" Julie called urgently.

Fears of vengeful gunmen leapt into my head as we hurried to see what was going on. The roar of the motorbike drew closer as Pete Hogan rode into view. Getting closer, I could see he had someone on his pillion. He pulled up beside the coach, took off his helmet, and threw it to the ground, shaking his long hair loose. He was pale, and his hair stuck to his sweating face.

Wincing, he fumbled at his chest, trying to release the bungee cord wrapped around his body that held his passenger to him. Charlie and Sean hurried forward to help. Gently, they

took the leather-clad rider and laid him on the ground. Murmurs flitted among the onlookers. Grunting, Pete got off his bike; his leather coat was soaked in blood and bullet holes were in the bike's exhaust pipe and rear mudguard.

"I couldn't leave him," Pete said apologetically. "I just ... couldn't," his voice cracked.

I looked at him and then, in wonder, I looked down on the body of Roger Boulton.

Twenty

SCOTLAND

I loved Scotland. It was hard, tough, and beautiful. The mountains were unforgiving and the terrain rough. In the Highlands, it was continually wet and raining and often very cold. We brought Roger to his new home and buried him on the border between England and Scotland on a high bank of the River Sark. There was no coffin. He was sewn into a thick waterproof tarpaulin and dressed in his full biker leathers. His head rested on his old helmet; the ice blue helmet had been lost at the ambush site. His motorcycle was parked at the head of the grave in lieu of a stone—a fitting tribute. He would have liked that. The funeral was sombre. Very little was said, but it raised the morale of the family to know that we had laid Roger to rest with love and affection—the wrong made right. It went a long way to alleviate the hurt we all felt in our hearts.

The land was ostensibly clear of vines, though not entirely. A few sickly feeble specimens struggled for existence; they lost their struggle against the fire we used to eradicate them. There was no sign of any Creeps.

We crossed into Scotland, passing a road sign depicting the flag of St. Andrew, a white cross on a light blue field. It was far from the triumphant conclusion to our journey that I had imagined so many times. Turning west, the convoy headed for the Highlands just as night began to fall. That first night was quiet; each of us was lost in our own private thoughts, and I didn't doubt for a second that Jules and Roger were featured in every one.

The one redeeming factor was that it wasn't so hot here. The temperature was higher than normal, but there was still a chill in the air which was a relief from the incessant heat down south. I figured the farther west we went into the mountains, the cooler it would get.

Everyone was awake just after first light. Breakfast was prepared, and people were a little chattier this morning after a clearly restless night for all. I had heard the two motorcycles roar off just before dawn, fading into the encroaching morning light. I hadn't even felt Linda get out of our makeshift bed.

Despite the gloom hovering over the camp, I heard several awestruck comments about the surrounding countryside: the mountains looming majestically to the west, the clear, sweet smelling air redolent with the scent of pine, the clear, cold water of the bubbling stream rushing past our camp. Thankfully, people's spirits began to rise. Even Tina had left the confines of the coach and was sitting wrapped in a blanket with Sally and Little Eve, enjoying the beautiful scenery around us.

Linda and Peter had been ranging far ahead, checking out the area. Four hours later they returned, both looking as pleased as punch. They had discovered a small village with no more than fourteen stone-built houses surrounding a kirk about fifteen miles away in a sheltered glen. Exploration proved it would do for now. And should we decide to stay there, the village offered ample opportunity for expansion; there was ample timber from a small wood in the next valley available for building new houses when needed. Excited chatter rippled through the family as Linda told us the news, and Sean was already voicing plans for construction. We broke camp in record time; everyone was eager to see their new home for themselves.

It was beautiful. The village was situated at the mouth of a low valley next to a fast-running stream that meandered down from the mountains. It fed the village's water supply which, with a little work, we would soon have running again to every house. The temperature was still significantly higher than normal. Scotland might not see snow again for a considerable amount of time—if ever. But that was good. The melting snow remaining on the high mountains would contribute to maintaining our stream.

Wide open fields surrounded us. They were somewhat overgrown with grasses and brambles, but that would be easy enough to remove. Tom and his boys had checked, there was no sign of the vines. Jeff and Alan were studying maps of the area taken from the last small services we passed as we left the motorway. They

hoped it would give them some idea where to look for farm machinery, tractor sales, or anything that could help us. If anyone could find such things, it was them. They were doing what they did best.

The kirk was designated as home for Tricia, Joan, and the children. Hilda seemed to have made the adjustment from her Harmony persona and was proving to be a valuable asset, so much so that she acquired the nickname "Hilly," signalling that she was going to be accepted into our family—the past forgotten. In time, even Terry began to warm to her as the real woman revealed herself.

Linda and I took a small house on the edge of the village. It didn't take her long to make it warm and comfortable. Working together, we cleaned the place top to bottom, which wasn't as dirty as one might expect after standing empty for so long. The furniture was basic and very usable; the bed frame was solid, and the firm mattress was given a good beating and fumigation before we actually slept on it. New linen and towels were taken from our stores. There was no electricity; it was one of the three houses that didn't. Sean took the second house, and Terry and Teresa took the third. The three generators were used to power the rest and the kirk. Tom Taylor promised to have us connected to an electric supply as soon as possible.

The children loved this place with no name. Predictably, it was called "Eden," which was alright. It sheltered below a large rocky outcropping. A panorama spread out before us; fields rolled up to the blue shrouded mountains which glittered in the sun. The place was idyllic.

It was more than I could ever have hoped for, and doubts and fears melted away like the snow on the mountaintop. We quickly settled in.

There was enough food to last us for months, and with Jeff and Alan scavenging, none of us would go hungry. I was sure of that. Plans were laid to plant fields with everyone deciding what crops should be grown. Linda and Pete promised to help our scavengers in the hunt for farm equipment.

As a first project, Sean suggested that we renovate the inside of the kirk. It basically consisted of a very large hall and two small anterooms which Trish and Joan had commandeered as private rooms. The kids were sleeping in a makeshift dormitory, so Sean thought a little privacy was in order and intended to create small bedrooms with stud partitioning, giving each room a window so the children wouldn't feel as if they were in prison cells. The only thing lacking at the kirk were bathroom facilities, but with the help of some of the other men, Sean built a large bathroom extension with several toilets to accommodate the throng.

Another great surprise was the large boxes of seeds and grain Jeff and Alan produced: vegetables, herbs, corn, and maize. We laughed when we noted the oats, what was Scotland without porridge? Plus several boxes of flower bulbs, though they confessed they had no idea what flowers.

One small event of note was when Wei Lin, ever adventurous, got stuck up a tree and was unable to get down. Trish had been sitting outside her cottage playing with Eve when Wei

began screaming for help. Hastily, Trish put the baby into her wickerwork cradle and hurried to rescue Wei. The youngster was finally persuaded by Sean to jump from the branch which was barely three feet above the big Irishman's head; he assured her that he would catch her. Amid cheers and cries of encouragement, Wei Lin jumped and everyone cheered again. The excitement over, everyone went back to what they had been doing. Approaching her cottage, Trish stopped in her tracks and called quietly to Sally, who called equally softly to me and Linda, pointing toward Tricia's house.

And there was Tina, dressed for the first time since we had left the Block in light coloured slacks and a bright red pullover; she was holding baby Eve and laughing.

In just under three weeks, we were established. Our new life had begun. Our family was happy, and for the first time in a long time, our future looked bright.

"It's beautiful here," Linda said as we walked arm in arm along the rocky ridge overlooking Eden.

"We were lucky," I said, looking out toward the mountains to the west.

The day was fine; only a few white clouds scuttled across an otherwise clear blue sky as evening came on. Deep purple edged the distant horizon.

"I had all sorts of misgivings about coming here," I admitted. "I had visions of finding the country overrun and us trying to get across the North Sea to Norway or something."

Linda laughed. "You made the right choice, and Norway would have been a viable option if Scotland proved to be a bust. We could have gone to Aberdeen, grabbed a boat…"

"Not sure if we could have managed a boat either; I'm not fond of the sea," I said with a smile. "And Norway would have been a lot harder. Thankfully, we landed on our feet."

"The kids like it here," Linda said brightly. "So does everybody else. We have all we need to make this place secure and productive. We're home, Adam."

The others were sitting around the cliff top, talking and laughing; the children were enjoying playing ball with some of the older kids. We had suspended work for the afternoon and held an impromptu picnic overlooking our new home. It was laid out before us like a jewel in the sun, nestled in the valley at the foot of a range of majestic mountains with a glimmer of snow still on their rugged shoulders.

I left Linda talking with Julie and Charlie and wandered closer to the cliff's edge to enjoy the view and have a few quiet moments alone. Passing a clump of rocks, I smiled down at the stream running past Eden, glittering like a silver thread across the verdant landscape, rolling down out of the mountains with crystal clarity. Heather and pine from the nearby forest was redolent on the warm air, insects buzzed nature's eternal litany, and a soft, gentle breeze lifted my hair from my neck and shoulders and cooled me. I closed my eyes and enjoyed the sensation.

Linda was right: I was home.

I don't know what made me turn at that precise moment—instinct maybe or some sort of subconscious warning. Regardless, I turned just in time to see a dark shape hurtling toward me, seemingly from out of the sky. Instinctively, my arm came up to ward off a blow that never came. Instead, a set of powerful jaws clamped over my forearm and sharp vicious teeth ripped flesh.

I screamed, crashing onto the stony ground as my attacker landed on top of me and pounded me mercilessly with a clawed fist. I struggled, beating at the hairy brute with my right hand. I pummelled its ribs, sides, and head to no effect. Something wet and warm splashed onto my face—my blood. I tasted the salty iron in my mouth. Still screaming, I heaved sideways, and we tumbled apart.

Rolling, I came unsteadily to my feet. My vision was blurred and my head reeled from the appalling pain roaring through my body. My left arm hung mangled and useless at my side; the hand didn't seem to be a part of me, hanging at an unnatural angle to the wrist. Blood flowed in torrents, soaking the ground.

Twenty feet away, the Creep crouched, its red eyes blazing, claws scratching at the solid rock, and drool hanging in ropes from its gnashing jaws that were stained pink with blood—my blood. With a shock, I recognised the clump of black fur shaped like a lightning bolt running across the brute's deep chest. Its right claw was missing, leaving only an ugly scarred and burned stump. My heart froze. It was impossible, but here it was—the Creep I had mutilated on the Queen Elizabeth Bridge so many weeks ago.

Sobbing, I used my good hand to ease the ruined left arm into the front of my shirt; immediately the material was stained crimson. Tugging my knife from its sheath and holding it awkwardly in my right hand, I faced the monster.

"Come on then, you son-of-a-bitch, come and get it..."

My head was reeling from the poison in the Creep's saliva rushing through my veins—already doing its evil work. I thought I heard someone shouting behind me, but the blood thundering in my ears blocked out all sound. With terrifying speed, the Creep lunged at me. Screaming, I slashed with the knife; once, twice, the razor-sharp blade sliced through flesh. Howling as its teeth sank into my right shoulder, we rolled on the ground. I was oblivious to the sharp stones gashing at my back. I stabbed and stabbed and stabbed as my breath came in huge gasps.

Claws ripped across my stomach as we came perilously close to the edge of the cliff. The brute had me pinned, and my strength was diminished. Feebly, I lashed out with the knife as the Creep reared up, cavernous maw gaping. With my hair tangled in its clawed fist, it pulled my head inexorably back, exposing the soft flesh of my throat. Spiders skittered across my brain, invading my mind with their loathsome touch—the Creep's horrendous, noiseless scream.

Desperate madness gave me strength and with one last surge, I heaved and twisted my

tortured body and stabbed my knife upward. There was a brief sensation of falling. Dimly, I realised we had gone over the edge of the cliff. The world exploded with jarring suddenness; I didn't even have time to scream as blackness swallowed me.

ENDS.

Book Club Questions

1. Linda reappears at the end of *JUNGLE* and at the beginning of *HELL'S ROAD*. She has drastically changed. Do you think someone can change that much in ten months? (Bearing in mind we have no back story for Linda at this point.)

2. England basically became a military state. Would this be enforceable?

3. With most of the United Kingdom's population dead, what would be the point in a military state?

4. Jules Robideaux is the oldest member of the "Family," their mentor, their guiding hand. Was his death gratuitous?

5. At the motorway services at Newport Pagnell, the "Family" is attacked by scavengers. Is this a trope? A cliché? (ie: *Mad Max: Fury road. The Road, The Book of Eli*.)

6. Was "Harmony Quaid" (Hilda Quinlen) a feasible character?

7. The Creeps are evolving, becoming more intelligent, bigger. Do you think they are more frightening being more

intelligent, or should they remain essentially bestial?

8. I have tried to minimise the use of firearms as I personally hate guns. Would survivors in a dangerous dystopian world use guns more readily other than for hunting food? To kill another human being, especially when most of the world's population has died is a terrible loss.

9. At the end of *HELL'S ROAD*, Adam is attacked by a vengeful Creep and severely mauled. Both Creep and Adam tumble over a sheer precipice. The question is, should Adam die?

Author Bio

Alan Berkshire was born in London, United Kingdom in the year of who-knows-when.

As the seventh child in a family of thirteen children, he has lived a full and happy life, enjoying the outdoors, camping, travelling, painting, and writing.

Residing in Austin, Texas, since November 2017, he looks forward to a long and fruitful writing career and is happy to present Hell's Road, the second book in his Jungle Series.

More books from
4 Horsemen Publications

Fantasy, SciFi, & Paranormal Romance

Beau Lake
The Beast Beside Me
The Beast Within Me
Taming the Beast: Novella
The Beast After Me
Charming the Beast: Novella
The Beast Like Me
An Eye for Emeralds
Swimming in Sapphires
Pining for Pearls

D. Lambert
To Walk into the Sands
Rydan
Celebrant
Northlander
Esparan
King
Traitor
His Last Name

Danielle Orsino
Locked Out of Heaven
Thine Eyes of Mercy
From the Ashes
Kingdom Come

J.M. Paquette
Klauden's Ring
Solyn's Body

The Inbetween
Hannah's Heart
Call Me Forth
Invite Me In
Keep Me Close

Lyra R. Saenz
Prelude
Falsetto in the Woods: Novella
Ragtime Swing
Sonata
Song of the Sea
The Devil's Trill
Bercuese
To Heal a Songbird
Ghost March
Nocturne

T.S. Simons
Antipodes
The Liminal Space
Ouroboros
Caim
Sessrúmnir

Ty Carlson
The Bench
The Favorite

DISCOVER MORE AT
4HORSEMENPUBLICATIONS.COM